Gia in the City of the Dead

Gia Santella Crime Thrillers, Volume 1

Kristi Belcamino

Published by Kristi Belcamino, 2017.

YOUR FREE BOOK IS WAITING

"Keep your eye on this writer" - Lisa Unger, NYT bestselling author

When they made fun of her family in school, she learned karate to fight back.

But now her skills had failed her.

The attack--from someone she trusted--changed her, and her life, forever.

She was alone in the world and it was up to her to seek her own justice.

Vendetta was her destiny.

Find out more at the end of Gia and the City of the Dead

GIA IN THE CITY OF THE DEAD

By Kristi Belcamino

CHAPTER ONE

NORTH BEACH, SAN FRANCISCO

I eyed the brunette in the sparkly underwear as she whipped her long hair and draped her tanned legs around the silver pole, sliding one stiletto-heeled foot up and down, up and down.

Her breasts, naked and swinging, were bigger than mine, but she was about the same size and weight. No stretch marks. Hips still slim. Childless. No thin white band on her ring finger. Single. Fake diamond studs. Not doing this for fun or to rebel against daddy. Fuchsia toenail polish. Definitely *not* from the Bay Area. Perfect white teeth and flawless skin. Not a crankster. No identifying tattoos.

She would do.

I slid three twenties under the strap of her G-string and told her to meet me in the private room at her break.

Waiting in the tiny, mirrored room, I rummaged around in my bag for a roach, but came up empty. Must have smoked it last night. At the bottom of my purse, my fingers brushed some loose shake so I licked them and stuck them back into my bag. I poked around until tiny green flecks stuck to the pads of my fingers, which I licked again. I was plucking a few stray flakes off my lipstick when she walked in, wiping tiny beads of sweat away from her temple with a small white towel.

She leaned back against the door and untied her short silky robe.

"Hey, honey. What's your name?" she asked, fluffing her hair. My back was to her, but I didn't take my eyes off her face in the mirror.

"Gia," I said and smiled. Yes, she would do perfectly.

"I'm Candy." *Sure you are.* She sidled up to me, pressing her bare breast against my arm from behind, trailing her fingers down my arm as we watched ourselves in the floor-length mirror.

"It's not what you think," I said, gently pushing her away.

Ten minutes later we had a deal.

I slipped back into the night, ignoring the groups of men huddled on the neon sidewalks outside, smoking and cat calling everyone who looked like they might have a vagina—whether they were born that way or not.

CHAPTER TWO

THE PREVIOUS WEEK ...

The throbbing head pain keeping time with my heartbeat told me last night had been a doozy. Even if I didn't remember any of it.

Without opening my eyes, I knew it was time to get up because I could hear the noisy gurgling of my Nespresso in the kitchen. The espresso machine was programmed to kick on at two every afternoon so that when I rolled out of bed hot coffee would be waiting. It was a rough life.

If I got dressed quickly, I could still make it to a Budo session at my dojo before I had to go see my godfather in Monterey. I stretched and yawned and then froze at the sound of clanging in my kitchen.

As I yanked the covers up over my naked breasts and reached under my huge stack of pillows for my gun, a vague memory surfaced — a cute face, tight ass, and deft hands. I'd brought some guy home from the bar last night. I groaned. He should've been long gone. I put the gun back. If he was banging pots and pans around in the kitchen, he probably wasn't a serial killer.

A curly-haired head peeked around the doorframe. "Hey, Gia. You hungry? It'll be ready in a jiffy."

I stared until his head withdrew. He whistled as he walked back to the kitchen. Jiffy? Whistling? That did it. This guy was way too polite and chipper to be my type. I closed my eyes trying to piece together what had happened the night before. I vaguely remembered Scott, the bartender at Anarchy, refusing to fill my glass again despite me wadding up hundred dollar bills and throwing them at him. How much had I had to drink? It must have been a lot because Scott had never cut me off before. The last thing I remembered was stomping off to find someone else to order my booze for me.

I must have found the guy who was now in my kitchen.

He seemed harmless. I shrugged on my kimono and tried to avoid looking into the mirrored doors on my closet as I walked past, but still managed to get a glimpse of a green-silk-robe-wearing witch with wild hair.

I stopped in the bathroom to splash some water on my face, again avoiding the mirror. I glanced into the small metal trash can near the toilet.

Terror streaked through me when I didn't see a neatly tied up condom inside. I dumped the contents, tissue paper, cotton balls, eyeliner pencil shavings onto the white tile floor, heart pounding, and knelt down. On my hands and knees, I combed through the debris. Nothing. I even stooped down and looked behind the toilet. He could have flushed it. But probably not.

In my bedroom, I flopped down on my white sheepskin rug and looked under the bed with a flashlight. I searched every corner of the room. I stuck my gun in my nightstand and tore all the covers off the bed, tossing the duvet, sheets and pillows across the room.

Still, nothing.

The whistling from the kitchen made me wince.

Time to face my houseguest.

I leaned on the doorframe leading into my small kitchen. The guy was putting slices of sourdough bread in my toaster. Eggs and milk were on the counter. Butter was sizzling in a frying pan on the stove. The guy *was* cute. But none of that mattered. I cleared my throat. He looked up and smiled.

"Listen ..." I closed my eyes for a second. *Did we have full-on intercourse? Did we use a condom?* I was too humiliated to ask. "I'm sure you're really sweet. But you have to leave now."

When I opened my eyes, his smile had faded. I tried again. "I drank a lot last night. It's better if you leave. Now."

"Hey, I'm a feminist," he said, holding his palms out. "I don't take advantage of drunk women. If anything, you talked me into coming back here. I kept saying it probably wasn't a good idea, but you insisted otherwise. You practically dragged me home."

I cringed. He was probably right. But I still needed to get rid of this nameless, chivalrous stranger. "Like I said," I began again. "You seem like a really nice guy. But you need to go." *Did we have sex?* I couldn't make my lips form the words.

"No problem." He didn't seem angry, only disappointed, maybe even a little hurt. For a brief second I felt a twinge of guilt, but quickly dismissed it. I needed to get this stranger out of my house immediately. Before I freaked the fuck out.

He grabbed a leather jacket off my dining room table. I noticed an empty wine bottle and two glasses on the table along with what looked like the remains of a pumpkin pie. Guess I had brought the party back here.

When the door finally clicked closed, I sunk onto the chair on my balcony with a cup of espresso and a pack of Dunhills. I felt another stab of guilt remembering the guy's face when I told him to leave. For a split-second I wondered if I should have gotten his name, in case ... No, I wasn't going to go there. For now, I was going to assume that we *hadn't* had full-on sex. It would be odd for me, but not totally unheard of. He seemed like a good guy. I know I'd made him feel bad by kicking him out, but what else was I going to do?

Besides I had a date with the godfather today. Something I was both looking forward to and dreading. Apparently, Vito had a favor to ask me. Something he could not tell me over the phone. My stomach knotted thinking about it and the trip to Monterey. Ever since my parents died, any visit home brought a flood of painful memories.

As a result, I usually ended up drinking too much and having to stay over in the guesthouse of my godfather's Carmel home.

Of course, I could always stay at my parents' house, which Vito had made sure had been kept like a pristine mausoleum since their deaths two years ago.

But in my mind, the house loomed like an eerie specter. I wasn't afraid of ghosts. However, I was terrified of walking into my childhood home, once filled with my mother and father's laughter and conversation, and finding it hollow and empty. That would flatten me.

The house needed to be sold. I know I could never live there. And my brother, Christopher, had vowed to never return to the Monterey Peninsula during his lifetime. An hour after my parent's funeral, Christopher got in his car and before he pulled away told me I would never see him on the peninsula again. And that if he died unexpectedly, he didn't want to be buried in the family plot.

"Cremate me and then do whatever the hell you want with the ashes. Leave them at the funeral home for all I care. As long as it's not in Monterey. Promise me." He stared at me until I agreed. Then he pulled away.

Watching the tail lights of his Bugatti pull away, I'd crossed my arms and thought, "Sure, I'll cremate you and then flush you down the god damn toilet."

It was the last time I'd seen him. As far as I knew, he had kept his promise to never return to the peninsula.

Ever since we were kids, he'd hated living on the peninsula. It was his own fault. He was cruel and antisocial and was ostracized by most of the other kids. I think that's why my parents ultimately sent him away to boarding school. I couldn't count on him to help me clean out my parent's house or sell it. It was up to me.

Until I could bring myself to sort through my parent's belongings, it would remain frozen in time. Deep down inside I knew I needed to face it sooner or later.

My crotch itched slightly and a streak of terror zipped through me again. I had always been exceedingly careful in my one-night stands, but I still couldn't find a god damn condom from last night. All I could do was hope and pray that we hadn't actually had sex. The curly-haired guy had even said, "I don't take advantage of drunk women." For some reason his decency made me feel even worse for kicking him out.

I took a drag off my cigarette and gulped my coffee, consoling myself with the thought that he was too nice and therefore too good for me, anyway. I'd actually probably done him a favor by booting him out before he started to really like me.

I spent at least an hour sitting on my balcony, feet up on the rail in my fuzzy slippers, watching the fog burn off the bay until the Golden Gate Bridge came into view and beyond that the Marin headlands. If I looked over my shoulder, I could see the new span of the Bay Bridge stretching across the Bay, gleaming in the sunlight.

Even though a lump of dread had settled in my gut, the trip to the Monterey Peninsula would be good for me. It was one of those days where I needed to drive my Ferrari as fast as I could for as long as I could.

CHAPTER THREE

AS SOON AS MY RED FERRARI hit the open highway headed south of San Francisco, I let her loose. I firmly pressed my Giuseppe Zanotti stiletto-heeled sandal to the floor as I watched my speedometer soar. I cranked the Gorillaz and zipped around slower cars, only easing up when the speedometer hit 100 mph on the curves.

My hair was whipping in the wind and would end up a tangled knot before I slowed down, but I could care less. Driving this way sent a rush of adrenaline through me. The freedom of the open road was one of the few things that soothed my soul. A little bit south of San Francisco I turned down the radio. "Dial Dante."

I heard him fumbling as he answered the phone. "*Ciao bella, mi amore*."

"I miss you."

"Me too," he said. "You on your way?"

Dante ran a little restaurant in Calistoga. We'd been best friends since high school — two misfits in the clique-y WASPish Carmel world where Italian-American kids were looked down on and even a little bit feared.

"No. I've been summoned to the peninsula. By Vito. Had to miss my session at the dojo."

He was quiet for a second before he spoke. "What about?"

"I don't know."

I could tell he heard the worry in my voice I had tried to hide. "Do you think his health has taken a bad turn?"

Dante always said what I was afraid to say out loud.

My silence was his answer.

He cleared his throat.

"I should probably concentrate on the road," I said. "I just needed to hear a friendly voice."

I knew I sounded pathetic.

"Come up tomorrow, then."

"Okay."

I clicked off without saying goodbye.

I rolled into the Monterey Peninsula fog at around one. For most of the drive, I'd thought about my parent's house. I had to face my fear. It had been two years. It was time I looked inside.

My "appointment" with my godfather wasn't until two so I had time. At the last minute, I swerved and headed toward the gated community of Pebble Beach before I could change my mind.

At the entry to Pebble Beach at 17-Mile-Drive, I stopped at the guard post and rummaged around in my glove box for a few minutes before I unearthed my pass. When I finally triumphantly held it up to the guard he said, "Good day, Miss Santella" without even looking at it. I was a little miffed. If he knew who I was, why didn't he just wave me through?

My stomach was in knots by the time I pulled up to the gate at my old house, I punched in the old code I had as a child. When the gate opened, I wasn't sure if I was more disappointed than relieved it had worked.

I parked behind the large detached four-car garage, next to the once well-trod path through the trees to Dante's home. The trail was now overgrown with thick prickly bushes. As children, Dante and I'd spent many a summer day playing bandits in the wooded area between our two homes.

Later, when we were teenagers, we'd sneak Bacardi 151 and cigarettes to a clearing in the middle of the woods. We'd drink and smoke and talk about our dreams as we lay on the mossy ground and looked at the stars. It was on one of those stargazing nights I'd leaned over to kiss Dante and he'd confessed his dark secret — he was in love with my brother Christopher. I ran out of the woods and wouldn't talk to Dante for a week. I was crushed. Just like my mother had, Dante had chosen my sociopath brother over me.

I couldn't live without Dante, however, and quickly forgave him. I needn't have worried, though. Over Christmas break, something happened between them — I'll probably never know what —that ensured Dante would hate Christopher for eternity and be mine — if only as a friend — forever.

I cast one last glance at the overgrown path and felt a tug of nostalgia for my childhood. When I was little, it seemed like being surrounded by a family who loved me was my destiny. I had no idea it could all disappear and leave me alone in the world. Tough luck, kid, I said to myself, heading toward the house.

My Budo karate training had trained me not to wallow in self-pity.

We are but a small part of the whole and we must remember that our own fears and hurts and tragedies are crucial to make us who we are as we strive to become selfless. While our hurt is real, we must rise above them to reach warrior status. We take the pain and use it to grow stronger. We conquer our fears by facing them straight forward and render them powerless before us. We know that our ultimate purpose is not to serve selfishly, but to use our fears and struggles to become stronger so that we may help others less fortunate than us.

Time to Budo on up.

I held my key out before me at the front door. I was counting on it still working and it did. The large door swung open and I stepped inside, quickly closing it behind me before I changed my mind. I leaned back against the door, closed my eyes and inhaled. The house smelled like home. And then, suddenly, more than anything in the world, I wanted to bury my face in the smell of my mother. I dropped my keys and bag onto the floor and ran up the staircase. I didn't stop until I was in my mother's walk-in closet.

I ripped her neatly hung clothes off the teak hangers in a frenzy, pressing them to my nose and then throwing them on the ground if they didn't exude her Chanel perfume smell. It had been too long. They smelled like nothing. Finally, when nearly every item had been thrown on the floor, I collapsed, exhausted onto the heap of silk and wool clothing. I lay with my face buried in a pile of clothes sobbing until the stabbing pain in my gut turned into a dull feeling of emptiness. Finally, I rolled onto my back and looked around. That's when I saw it.

A notebook-sized panel in the wall. It was usually hidden by rows of hanging clothes. I ruined my manicure prying it open. Inside was a round vintage hat box papered in gold and silver foil. Nothing else.

I carefully pulled the hat box out, kicking aside the pile of clothes to clear a spot on the floor. I plopped down with the box and stared at the lid. Maybe my missing birth certificate was in there.

Over the years, whenever I'd needed a birth certificate, my godfather had stepped in and done something that prevented me from actually ever having to produce the document. I had never actually seen my birth certificate.

When I went to get my driver's license at the Monterey office of the Department of Motor Vehicles, Vito had come with me. Instead of waiting in line like I did once with Dante, we were taken to a back office where they processed everything and sent us on our merry way. I never even had to take a driver's test. At the time, I figured it was because I had passed three racing courses at Laguna Seca before I turned fifteen, but now I wondered.

I stared at the box for a few seconds, finally said, fuck it, and lifted the lid.

I was right. And wrong.

There weren't any snips of baby hair tied with a ribbon. The box only contained papers, letters and documents. Some were love letters, written in hard to read cursive. I picked up the first stack—saw they were signed by my father—and threw them back in the box. I knew someday I'd be ready to read more details about my parents' legendary love. Just not today.

I flipped through the other papers. Looks like some land deeds, titles or something for some property in Italy. I wasn't surprised to see my mother owned large swaths of land in Italy. My parents, together, had owned houses and property around the world, including a large villa on the Cinque Terre coast. Their favorite place to visit, however, had been their Lake Geneva mansion in Switzerland. The one that burned to the ground with their bodies inside.

The only thing surprising about that was that the land was solely in my mother's name. Some dude had given her all this land. It wasn't my grandfather, either. Some guy named Mateo Antonio Turricci. I wondered if he was the trustee for my grandparents' estate. But these deeds showed my mother as the sole property owner. All the land was in Sicily so it probably was her inheritance from her parents. It looked like some type of structure and acres of land.

I kept flipping through the papers. Then when I saw a seal on a document that I knew was a birth certificate, I got excited. But it was for my mother. I stared at her vital statistics and the cute little ink prints of her feet and it brought a thick sob to my throat. Beneath that was my brother, Christopher's birth certificate. I kept flipping through the papers. My dad's birth certificate wasn't in my mother's stash of precious papers. And neither was mine.

I swallowed. Just another small detail that made me feel unworthy and unloved. I knew my mother had loved me, but also knew she'd always loved Christopher more. It was a wound that would never heal.

I put the lid back on the box, disappointed. It was just normal official paperwork and sentimental shit anyone would save. I'd still keep the box, though. If it had been important enough to her to stash away in a secret location, then I'd keep it for her.

On the floor near the front door, I grabbed my bag and my keys. An envelope lay beside them that I hadn't noticed when I first came in. It was cream colored and had my mother's full name printed on it: Lucia-Grazia Bonadonna Santella.

It was odd to see her maiden name. In Italy, most women didn't take their husband's surname, but my mother had tried to be as American as she could. The letter didn't have any postage mark so someone must have slipped it through the mail slot in the door. Someone who didn't know she was dead.

The letter couldn't have been there long. My godfather said that Josie, the housecleaner who had worked for my mother for twenty years, still came to clean every Monday, so it had only been here a day. I tucked it into my purse and took one last look around. The house was spotless.

I slipped five hundred dollars out of my wallet and put it under a paper weight on a small table near the door with a small scribbled note that said, "For Josie."

I'll never forget meeting Josie's eyes at the graveside service. She was sobbing, wiping her face with the sleeve of her wool coat.

CHAPTER FOUR

MY GODFATHER, VITTORIO Domenic Guidi, lived across the street from Carmel Beach in a sprawling stone rambler with Bougainvillea plants spilling onto the sidewalk out front. I parked around the corner and knocked on the heavy oak door. His nurse opened it and smiled. "Gia, your godfather will be so happy to see you."

The nurse was a stunning redhead in her twenties who wore her hair back in a tight bun, a pencil skirt, and high-heeled pumps. She looked like a 50s pinup. She had a gentle but firm manner. I'm pretty sure she sweet-talked my godfather into doing everything she needed him to do. He couldn't resist a pretty face.

Today, she tugged on my arm to pull me into the house and then leaned over to whisper, "He had a rough night last night. I haven't given him a bath yet."

I was grateful my godfather was filthy rich so he could pay some sweet young nurse to bathe him now that he was ill.

Every time I visited Vito, he looked frailer. His MS was progressing faster than any of us had anticipated. It hurt so much to see my virile godfather—who, when I was a child, used to lift me up onto his shoulders in one fluid motion—as a weak elderly man. It was difficult to see him withering away. His brain was still sharp, which made the deterioration of his body even harder.

I found him in his wheelchair in the sunroom, doing a crossword puzzle with all the windows and French doors open to the lush garden of flowers that crept up the small hillside in his backyard. A large sunbeam streamed into the window and illuminated his face as he turned to smile at me.

"Gia!"

"Vito!" I rushed over, struck with dismay at how fragile he appeared. I leaned over and kissed his grizzly cheek, hiding my face for a few seconds. He was the only person left in the world who loved me and he was disappearing before my very eyes.

"Thank you for coming, Gia. I need your help."

My help? My godfather was the most powerful man I knew. Even in a wheelchair, he was all business. He didn't waste time getting to the point. His face was stern as he turned to me. "It's about your brother, Christopher."

An icy chill trickled through me.

Of course, I'd never remembered a time when my brother hadn't frightened me. The hatred in his eyes when my mother praised me. The vehemence that overcame him skinning the squirrels he shot in the woods behind our house. How he somehow got our live-in nanny fired after she told on him for watching her undress.

When Christopher was fourteen, he was sent away to boarding school in Germany. Within two years he was back home. It was all very hushed up, but I heard my parents talking. I overhead my father say that the headmaster was found dead, with his pants around his ankles and an ice pick through his eye. My mother was hysterical, crying that there was no way Christopher had anything to do with it. My father remained quiet.

Shortly after he returned home from Germany, Christopher was sent away again: this time to live with a family friend in Argentina. He was supposed to be working on a ranch. For whatever reason, he wrote me every week.

I never wrote back.

His letters were long rambling confessionals about his life in Germany and the girl he had fallen in love with there: Bridget.

She lived in the nearby village. But she would never let him see her house. They had met at the ice cream store one Saturday. Soon, they were sneaking out at night and meeting in a tiny fisherman's shack on a nearby lake.

But Bridget was damaged. Her mother turned a blind eye to ongoing sexual abuse by Bridget's stepfather. When she confessed this to Christopher one night, he promised to save her from her stepfather. He said he would go home with her right then and confront her stepfather, make him stop. But Bridget made him promise not to follow her home. It would destroy her mother, she said.

The more Christopher begged her to let him help, the more she drew away. She started hanging out with the rough kids in town and soon was injecting heroin into her veins. Still, Christopher thought he could save her. But he couldn't compete with Bridget's past and the pain it had caused her. He couldn't compete with her longing to forever escape from this world.

Christopher was the one who found her body one night, curled up in a ball in a corner of the shack by the lake. Her wrists slit.

It was only after her death that Christopher learned that Bridget's stepfather was the headmaster at his school. When he found out, nothing could stop Christopher in his fury and grief. It wasn't long after that the headmaster's body was found.

When I received these confessional letters in the mail, my blood would rush to my face and I would hide in my bedroom to read them. I wanted to scream and throw the letters at my mother, saying "Your precious son is a murderer!" But I loved her too much to destroy her. Plus, I couldn't help but wonder whether she might already know.

Soon, Christopher's letters to me grew nasty. He would address them to me as "Daddy's Little Girl." Soon, they stopped altogether.

I hadn't seen or spoken to Christopher since my parent's funeral.

Hearing my godfather bring him up sent a wave of apprehension racing through me. I knew Vito had no love for Christopher.

"What about Christopher?" I braced myself for what he would say next.

"He is an embarrassment to your family name."

"I know." I clamped my lips together. Even though we were adults, when my parents died, my godfather had taken on the role of our guardian in some ways. He was the executor of our parent's estate and was really the closest thing left to a family member.

Even though he'd never liked Christopher, I think he wanted to honor my mother's wishes to watch out for her beloved son. I waited for him to go on.

"He thinks now that he is a vampire or some other nonsense," Vito flapped his gnarled hand in disgust.

"What? Where is he?"

"Santa Cruz. Living with some street urchins or something, I don't know. I try not to pay attention, but when people come to me and say he is doing shameful things to young women, what can I do?"

I remembered that when I was growing up people who were obsessed with the movie The Lost Boys moved to Santa Cruz and pretended to be vampires. It was more of a cult than anything else. Sort of like cosplay, but more intense. I was surprised it was still going on, but not surprised my brother was involved. But it still creeped me out.

"What kind of things?" I realized I was holding my breath waiting for his answer. I thought about the headmaster with the ice pick in his eye.

"Things that in the old country would mean this." My godfather slowly drew one long finger across his neck. The gesture sent a tremor down my spine.

"You want me to talk to him?"

Vito stared at me. "I'm giving him one chance, for your mother's sake," he said. "If this doesn't work, I will have no choice."

The thought of seeing him again made my skin crawl. But he was my blood. In my world, you put *famiglia* first. My mother and father had raised me to respect and honor family above all others. Although Vito was as close as family, he still wasn't blood. *Il sangue non è acqua*—blood is thicker than water. My duty to Christopher was to warn him about Vito's threat. When he drew his finger across his neck, I knew it wasn't an idle gesture.

Vito stared out the window, his fingers fiddling with the newspaper on his lap and then he turned, his eyes somber. "Tell him that if I don't hear that he has stopped his depraved ways on his own, I will make him stop. He should have been locked up years ago, but your mother forbade it."

I vaguely remember my mother and Vito arguing once late at night about Christopher. But until now I hadn't realized that Vito wanted Christopher institutionalized and that my mother had prevented him. I wondered why my father hadn't been part of that conversation.

The last thing I wanted to do was see my brother. But I would. I would find him and talk to him for my mother's sake and for Vito.

"Vito," I said, taking his hand in both of mine. "I'll talk to him. I'll have him call you, okay?"

"Good girl, Gia. I know you are a woman of your word, like your dear mother, God bless her." He made the sign of the cross and then twisted the newspaper until it was a cylinder. I knew my parents' death still hurt him. Every time I went to visit my parents' graves, there were signs that my godfather had been there right before me—fresh yellow roses, my mother's favorite.

"Let's go eat some lunch. Concetta fixed ravioli and pork roast." Before he would let me wheel him into the dining room, he reached down and scribbled something on a corner of his newspaper, ripped it off and put it in my palm, patting my hand with both of his.

Christopher's address.

CHAPTER FIVE

BY THE TIME I GOT TO Santa Cruz the sun was setting to the west, casting everything in a hazy golden light. The address Vito had given me led me to a small shack with a ramshackle front porch. It was on a large weedy lot next to a motel.

I knocked on the door until my knuckles hurt. I tried to peer through the dirty windows, but heavy black curtains blocked my view. Finally, after I kicked the door a few times, a pale-faced boy with sensuous full lips, black jeans, and no shirt answered the door with a large yawn.

A slow smile spread across his face as he took me in from head to toe, taking in my black leather miniskirt, the buckled boots that stretched up to my thighs and my ripped, too tight Morphine T-shirt.

But I didn't have time for his admiration. I was in a hurry to give my brother Vito's message and then get out of town.

"Who are you? Where's Christopher?" I scowled.

He scratched his belly and yawned again. Then shrugged. "I'm Bobby. Don't know. He lives here, but I never see him during the day."

"You don't know where your housemate is?" My voice dripped antagonism and sarcasm.

"Listen, I just moved in last week. I barely know the dude." He cracked his knuckles. I stared, waiting.

Then he smiled. "I have to tell you—you don't seem like his type."

"What the hell does that mean?"

"You aren't simpering and dumb." That sounded about right. I stifled a smile.

"I'm his sister." I narrowed my eyes at him.

He cleared his throat and grew serious. "You're his sister?"

I chewed my lip and looked away. This was taking way too much time. "Not my fault."

He laughed and instantly got a point in his favor.

"I need to find him."

"Like I said, I just moved in here last week so I don't know him very well."

"You're lucky."

He raised an eyebrow. "Is there something I should know?"

"Probably." I said blowing out a big puff of air. If this guy didn't know my brother was bad news he would find out soon enough. "Now, where is he?"

"I really don't know. Honest. I'm meeting him at the Reverend Horton Heat show later. Around nine. I don't think he'll be back in town until then."

"I need to talk to him now." I knew I was pouting and sounded like a child. I drew back my shoulders to try to salvage some dignity.

The boy shrugged. "Sorry." He looked over his shoulder. "You hungry? I just made some lentils and brown rice."

Of course he did. I tilted my head, examining him.

"You've got to eat, right? Plus, you have a few hours to kill. He's not going to be back until nine. I know that. He said he was going somewhere his cell phone didn't work. The mountains around here ... spotty cell service, so probably up there somewhere." He yawned again and stretched his arms above his head.

I wasn't hungry. At least not for food. I eyed his smooth, tanned, hairless chest and followed the faintest trail of soft hair down to where it dipped into his jeans. He was beautiful. A slow smile spread across my face. "Looks like I have some time to kill."

I put my palm on his chest and pushed him inside the darkened house.

BOBBY LED ME BY THE hand through the crowd outside The Catalyst. He was a sweet boy. I wondered what was wrong with him — something had to be off for him to have moved in with my brother. At the very least he lacked the ability to sense a clear-and-present danger—in both me and Christopher. We both screamed "damaged" from miles away.

People snarled as Bobby wove his way through the crowd, holding my hand close so I was right behind him. I rolled my eyes at the angry faces that turned our way. I searched the crowd for Christopher.

A jolt ran through me when I spotted him. He'd always had that effect on me, even across a crowd. I held my breath as I took him in.

His black hair was bleached a shocking white blond. He'd lined his dark eyes with heavy kohl and wore a flowing white poet's blouse with tight black jeans and tall boots. He was surrounded by a group of vampire wannabes with white faces, red lips and black capes flowing behind them. The girl on his arm had her black hair pulled up on top of her head in a sexy, messy up-do. Her tiny rouge lips pouted at something Christopher was saying.

She was just his type: adoring and clueless. Or "simpering and dumb," as Bobby had said.

The girl turned to face him, reaching up and wrapping her arms around his neck, pressing her body close to his. When he leaned down to kiss her, I blushed at how obscene it seemed. He groped her as if they were alone, unclasping her black velvet cape and throwing it on the ground. A stunning blue tattoo of gothic bat wings sprawled across her ivory shoulders.

His smile was seductive, but even across the crowd I recognized the disdain in his gaze as he looked down on the girl.

As far as I knew my brother had only loved two people in his life: our mother and Bridget. He would never love another. I wanted to warn her. My Budo karate training had taught me to protect the innocent.

We look at the world the way a warrior would. We actively observe and seek to become aware and vigilant. We remain on guard and ready to fight for the purposes of good — in defense of life and liberty for ourselves and others. The warrior stands up for those who are weak, for the innocent, for the vulnerable.

Budo required that I warn her. But I knew it wouldn't matter.

"There they are," Bobby said with a hint of something odd in his voice. I wondered if he was afraid of Christopher. I wouldn't blame him. I let go of his hand as we approached my brother and went on ahead. I stood before my brother and waited until he moved the girl out from between us.

"Gia." Christopher's voice was flat, monotone. Just like his dead eyes.

"Can I talk to you? Privately." The girl, who stood off to his side, clinging to his arm possessively, glared at me. I felt sorry for her. From what my godfather had hinted at, she'd be lucky to escape his clutches with just a broken heart.

"Inside," he said. Then Bobby was at my side and put his arm around me. Christopher gave Bobby a look I couldn't read. Was it a warning or a threat? Christopher turned on his heel and the small crowd surrounding my brother followed. At the door, Christopher gave a nearly imperceptible nod and the doorman unsnapped the red rope.

We filed in, following Christopher, who headed to a slightly elevated large table in the corner with probably the best view in the place. Every other spot was taken but for some reason this table, with enough seats for Christopher's gang of vampire enthusiasts, was waiting. Christopher nodded at a security guard who briefly lifted his chin before walking away.

A waitress appeared at Christopher's side. Bobby sat down beside me but I quickly moved to a seat on the other side. He was playing with fire. I tried to give him a warning glance, but he wouldn't look my way, just stared at Christopher with a defiant lift to his chin. The vampire kids began ordering drinks.

Christopher looked at me from beneath slightly hooded eyes. "What do you want, Gia?"

"I said I need to talk to you. Alone." My voice was steel.

He stood. "This way."

I followed him through the crowd to the entrance to backstage. The security guard manning the entrance didn't even blink as Christopher and I strolled by. A long hallway led to a series of closed doors. Christopher opened one and gestured for me to enter first.

He plopped onto a ratty couch, opened his gothic ring and dipped a long pinky nail into it, holding a bit of white powder up to his nose.

"Want a bump?"

I ignored his outstretched hand.

"What? You too good for it now or something?"

"What's up with the vampire thing?" I asked.

"You wouldn't understand," he said and gave me a slow smile, which revealed pointy incisors that looked real. He watched me as he ran his tongue along his teeth. I kept my face deadpan. Vampire worship and emulation was so 1990s. Bored that he couldn't get a reaction, he shrugged and crossed his legs.

"What about that girl you're with? She seems sweet, innocent."

"Oh, she is." He looked down and swallowed and for a moment I again saw the little boy who worshipped my mother. He shook his head.

"So, are you just going to break her heart like every other girl since Bridget?"

He flew off the couch so quickly I shrunk back, heart pounding. He had his elbow against my neck and my back against the wall. His eyes were inches away from mine. "What kind of game are you playing?"

I didn't answer—just stared into his dead eyes.

"Don't ever fucking say her name again." He growled it through gritted teeth. I didn't answer, even though it would only take a slight movement to disable him with a kick to the crotch. I wanted him to calm down. When I didn't move or answer, he finally relaxed and sat back down.

"Besides Gia, don't you know we are cursed in love? There's no use in fighting it."

For a split second, my brother — the one my mother loved so much — appeared. He sounded like a normal person, like someone who was caring and rational. And then he was gone. He whirled and gave me a leer.

"So, what's new with you, Gia? Are you already bored in the big city? Come down here slumming."

"I came to give you a message," I said.

"What on earth are you talking about?" His voice was silky and seductive, but held a hint of warning, danger.

"You've got to knock your shit off, Christopher." He genuinely looked baffled. "With the girls," I said. "I don't know exactly what you are doing, but Vito said if you don't stop, he's going to stop it for you."

"Oh. That." He squirmed despite himself. Vito might be the only person in the world who intimidated Christopher. He still tried to pull off the tough guy act, though. "That old bag of bones? What's he going to do?"

"He said if he has to, he'll stop you himself."

Christopher managed a low laugh, but it was laced with the slightest hint of fear.

"If you stop whatever you're doing ... he'll leave you alone," I reached over to his hip and unclipped his cell phone. "Call him. Now.

He knows everything you do, Christopher. He knows it all. If you call him and tell him you'll stop, he'll leave you alone."

I leaned over him, holding out his phone.

"Oh, the perfect Gia, swooping in to save the day. The little Italian princess is so valiant in saving her brother. Well, fuck you."

I let out a long breath. "Just call him. This has nothing to do with me. The only reason I'm here is for our mother."

Fury swept across his face. "How precious." His voice was filled with venom. "Well I have news for you. Our mother is dead. Dead in the ground. She's not up in heaven looking down with pride at her little girl so if you're doing anything for her, you're a fool and wasting your time."

His words were like a punch to the gut. I closed my eyes for a second so I could regain my composure. The last thing I would do is show him any weakness.

To my surprise, he reached for the phone in my hand and dialed.

A few seconds later, he spoke. I remained standing over him, frozen, afraid if I moved he would change his mind.

"Okay, old man. I'll stop. For now." The conversation lasted less than five seconds. He hung up and slid his fingers along my bare thigh.

"Looking good, sis."

I slapped him across one smooth, chiseled cheek, but he didn't even flinch, only gave me another slow smile. I walked out without looking back.

In a near panic, I fought my way through the crowd that was madly hopping up and down to the Reverend Horton Heat. The squirming mass was illuminated sporadically by flickering lights from the stage, making me disoriented as I pushed toward the door. The air seemed to be sucked out of the club by the frenetic energy and I fought to breathe as I pushed my way through the sweaty, bopping bodies that were bumping me this way and that. Finally, I broke free and flung open the door to the fresh night air.

I put my hands on my knees to try to catch my breath. My entire body shook uncontrollably. Christopher always had that effect on me. It was terrible to realize, but as much as I hated him, a tiny part of me, deep down inside loved him. That's why it hurt so much. They say that love and hate are two sides of the same coin. Maybe the part of me that loved him came from my mother. Even if I despised him with every other part of my being, that small piece of me couldn't get rid of images of his beaming face when he was with my mother. She was his life.

Unfortunately, when she died, anything that kept him in line, toeing the boundaries of society, also seemed to have disappeared. I didn't know what he was up to in Santa Cruz, but the possibilities sent a chill through me.

My thoughts were interrupted by a blast of music as the door to the club opened. The next thing I knew Bobby had me pressed close against the wall, kissing me so fiercely it took my breath away. All thoughts of Christopher vanished. It was hard to believe I'd only met this boy a few hours ago. Usually all I wanted to do after sex was say goodbye and never see the guy again. But for some reason, I just wanted to crawl in this boy's pocket and go home with him. Finally, I pulled away and turned to go.

"Hey." He grabbed my hand and gently pulled me back to him. "Give me your number."

I shook my head. "I don't think that's a good idea." I looked away, down the street where the fog was rolling in from the ocean, making the street lights hazy orange. I didn't have time for a boy in my life. Especially not this one. The strength of my attraction to him was dangerous. Unwanted.

"Come on." His voice was soft, irresistible. He kissed the sides of my lips so gently, he nearly convinced me. I pulled away.

"I live in San Francisco." That should be enough of a deterrent.

"Great," he said, reaching down and slowly running his thumb over my lips. "I'm graduating from U.C. this year and moving to the city. I'll call you next summer when I move. Maybe you can show me around."

"You'll have forgotten me by then." My smile was teasing but I meant every word. A year was a lifetime.

He put his hands on both sides of my head and drew me in close, eyes searching mine. "I could never forget you."

It was a probably a mistake, but I scribbled my number on a scrap of paper. He'd forget about me in a year. I pressed the paper into his hands.

"Whatever you do, don't ever let my brother know I gave it to you."

I turned and walked away before he could answer.

CHAPTER SIX

MY DEBAUCHERY WORE heavy on me at the dojo the next morning. I was sluggish and lazy. My sensei, Kato, had no mercy. Not for the first time, I wondered if he somehow suspected what I'd done over the weekend. I respected him too much to ever let him see just how out-of-control my life sometimes got. But he seemed to have a sixth sense about him and knew when I had gone off the deep end.

Slipping into the well-lit wide open loft space of the Dojo instantly calmed me.

I'd been studying Budo karate for the last ten years. In high school, a cheerleader cornered me in the hall and called me a *Wop*, a *Dago*, a *Guinea Negro*. I started to walk away. But then she called my dad a greasy Italian.

I punched the girl in the face hard enough to give her a black eye before her friends tackled me, managing to give me a few cracked ribs before a teacher broke it up. In the emergency room, my dad told me he was hiring someone to come to our Pebble Beach home every day after school to teach me martial arts. He said I could pick the style I wanted to learn. I did a little research online and decided to study *kyokushinkaikan*, also known as Budo karate, because I liked its code of honor.

I'd copied my favorite passage about the honor code onto a slip of paper I kept in my wallet:

"It is the duty of a warrior, not only to protect one's life, but to protect one's spirit. Warriors must train their hearts along with their bodies so their spirit is fierce and invincible."

The other reason I chose Budo was because I read that knowing the art could mean this: *The destruction of an opponent with one blow.* It seemed so efficient.

I knew I was too arrogant to excel in karate the way I wanted to because so much of the Budo philosophy involved being humble and of gentle spirit. I was more attracted to the ass-kicking part. But deep inside I knew if I were ever going to grow to the skill level Kato was, I'd have to get my shit together mentally and spiritually and emotionally. Like Kato.

The first thing I'd done after I moved to San Francisco, after taking shooting lessons and getting a permit to conceal and carry, was research my new *dojo*. Kato was one of the best sensei in the nation. As soon as I learned about his dojo, I knew I wouldn't settle for any other one.

At first Kato told me his class schedule was full and started to walk away. In frustration, I did a half-hearted kick at the wall. With lightning speed, Kato caught my leg with hands that felt like bands of steel and gave me a look so fierce I nearly ran out the door. Instead, I looked him in the eye and confessed everything to him — that Budo had saved my life and that it was the only thing that was keeping me afloat. His eyes searched mine. He saw it was the truth.

He threw me a robe and we began training that day.

Kato was in his forties and a firm, but gentle task master who commanded respect by his presence alone. He kept his sleek black hair longer in the back and his toned and fit body put Michelangelo's David to shame. It was no surprise that many of his students had crushes on him.

Today, Kato must have sensed I needed some guidance because he worked me twice as hard as he usually did, telling me to concentrate and pushing me until I was begging for a break.

I rarely sweat, Kato worked me so hard that by the time he let me take a break I had rivulets of perspiration dripping down my temple. I gulped down two bottles of water and wrapped a wet towel around my neck.

Kato wasn't even breathing hard. He sat down beside me. "Got plans later? Susie is making your favorite."

"Oh man, I promised Dante I'd come up for lunch." I guzzled my water, ignoring how some of it dribbled down my chin.

"Susie and the boys are going to be disappointed," Kato said, handing me a clean white towel.

"Not as much as I am," I said and grinned, wiping my face. "Tell her thanks. I'll stop by sometime next week. I need my Susie fix."

Kato was one of my favorite people in the world, but I loved his wife, Susie even more. She grew up in Berkeley, raised by two old hippies. She was a stay-at-home mom who baked her own bread, grew her own vegetables, and made her own granola. She wore her long hair in pigtails, wore armfuls of jangly bracelets, and dressed in flowing skirts that brushed the ground. She pretty much exuded the Zen that Sensei Kato taught his students.

Kato and his family lived in a rougher area of the Mission but were close with all their neighbors. His two little boys called me *Gia-Ko*, a riff off of *Gai-Ko*, which roughly translates to a derogatory form of "Westerner/Non-Japanese." They think the pun is hysterical. Even Kato smothers his smile when they say this, but when Susie — who is usually so mellow — caught them saying that once, she chased them around the house with a dishtowel. I hugged Kato goodbye. "Tell Susie I'll take a raincheck. And I'll bring the wine."

After I got home and showered, I retrieved my Ferrari out of the garage and pointed it north.

The drive to Calistoga was cathartic. Not as soul freeing as cruising Highway One south, but still it felt good to roll down all my windows and sing along to Beck's Odelay at the top of my lungs with my hair blowing wild.

Traffic was light. Not many people were heading north on a Monday.

"Dial Dante," I said once I passed Santa Rosa.

"Yo, what's your ETA, *paesana*."

"Be there in thirty." I hung up and cranked up the Beastie Boys, singing along.

Eighteen minutes later, I pulled into Buena Sera's parking lot. The white-washed walls of the restaurant were surrounded by purple, blue, and red flowers on vines and in big pots.

Dante was waiting for me outside at a shady table under a trellis of grape vines. He stood when he saw my car. Even from across the parking lot, the white of his smile against his olive skin made my stomach flip flop. Today he was wearing white linen pants and a white shirt with the buttons done enough for me to see his smooth, tan chest. And once again it was clear I would forever be half in love with him. But I knew deep having him for my best friend was worth more than anything else on God's green earth. Except maybe if I could bring my parents back to life.

He met me at the entrance to the outdoor dining area and grabbed me in a tight hug. I sniffed and he pulled back, searching my eyes. "Everything okay?"

I nodded and made my way to the table where a chilled bottle of Prosecco waited along with some prosciutto-wrapped cantaloupe slices.

"As soon as I see you, everything seems right in the world," I said, folding myself into the white metal chair and putting my sandaled feet up on the chair adjacent to me. "Maybe I should just move and be your busboy, girl, whatever they're called. Hell, I'd even wash your dishes."

"Gia, you know you'd go crazy up here. You're a city girl. You've always been one. That's why living in Monterey was so hard for you, remember *mia cara*?"

As a teenager, I'd get so restless that I'd break things in my room and cry and shout and then before I knew it, Dante would be out front in his beat-up, decades old Porsche 911 and he'd drive me up to Santa Cruz where we'd spend the evening watching punk rock bands. That soothed me for a little while, but then we'd have to go back to Carmel and Pebble Beach and Pacific Grove. The Monterey Peninsula was, as the saying goes, "a great place for the newly wed or the nearly dead," but for a teenager like me, it was soul crushing.

Dante and I settled in at the outdoor table and I leaned back in my chair, relaxed. The waiter brought a glass of Pinot Grigio and some tomato and basil bruschetta. I didn't complain. I'd already scarfed down the cantaloupe and was eager for more food.

"How's Matt?" I said, helping myself to a third bruschetta. Matt was Dante's long-time boyfriend. I'd grown to love him nearly as much as Dante.

"He's great. He's in D.C. right now."

Matt was a newly elected U.S. senator who would now split his time between Calistoga and D.C. I'd forgotten the session had just started. "You getting out there soon?"

Dante's face lit up. "Next weekend. Can't wait. It's only been a few days, but I miss that guy. More than I thought."

"He's a keeper, all right," I said.

"Hey!" Dante said, slapping the iron table with his palm. "I have a great idea! Why don't you come with me? Matt's got a huge townhome. He'd love to see you. I know you've always wanted to go to D.C. We can stay over an extra day and go exploring."

The thought of all the museums was tempting — the Smithsonian, the International Spy Museum, and the National Portrait Gallery. But it wasn't a good idea. I didn't want to be a third wheel, no matter how much they told me I wouldn't be.

"Maybe next time," I said.

"I tried to call you back the other night," Dante said. That's when I remembered leaving drunken messages for him from the bar at Anarchy. He looked hurt.

I cleared my throat. "Well, I was busy." He knew what I meant. His forehead scrunched up. He didn't like my casual sex life. He closed his eyes and let out a big sigh. "I've been patient and tried to be understanding about the way you're dealing with your parents' death, Gia. But I can't keep quiet any longer. Matt and I talked about this the other day and we agreed. You need to hear this. I love you and I can't watch you destroy yourself anymore. There's more to life than being high and fucking pretty boys." He looked at me.

I gulped and looked down into my drink. I had no answer. He was right.

When I first moved to San Francisco right after my parents died two years ago, I enrolled in art school believing I was following my dreams finally at age twenty. I even organized protests across the city in my spare time. But then the careful façade I had built around my grief crumbled and I found myself skipping class after all-night drinking sessions and then ultimately dropping out.

Since then I spent my time buying expensive shit I didn't need, getting shit faced and sleeping around. Each night blurred into the next. I'd usually end up both drunk and stoned if I was able to score some pot. Unfortunately, none of these activities ever took away the constant reminder that I was alone in this world — an orphan. I had no family anymore. My brother Christopher didn't count.

"Listen, Gia. This isn't like you. What happened to the Gia I knew who scoffed at all the other girls in high school who wore designer clothes?" He pointedly looked at my red-soled Louboutin stilettos. They'd cost $1,500 but were practically one of a kind. They were turquoise studded with turquoise spikes. They were kick ass. "What happened to the Gia who dreamed of joining the Peace Corps? Or the girl who talked about finding true love? Do you think this is how your parents would want you to grieve them? It's been two years, Gia. You are twenty-three years old. It's time to move on."

I stood up so quickly my chair toppled over, but I didn't turn around, just kept walking.

"Are you crying?" Dante yelled behind me.

When I got to my car, I rummaged in my bag for my keys. *Fuck. He was right. Fuck.* Coming here was a mistake. His disappointment stung. My vision was blurry, making it nearly impossible to find my keys. I crouched down, dumping my purse contents out on the ground until I saw them. I shoveled assorted lipsticks, concealers, spare pens, and old cough drops back in my bag.

When I stood, Dante was there. He grabbed me in a bear hug and buried his face in my shoulder. "Gia, I'm sorry for upsetting you. But I'm not sorry for saying what I did. I love you too much to sit back and let you destroy yourself. Will you please come sit back down?"

"I got a date. I gotta go." It was true. I did have a date, but I was also trying to avoid the pity I saw in Dante's eyes. I started to turn. Dante reached out and pulled me toward the restaurant.

"It's only four. You have time. Tell me about him?"

I looked at Dante's open, happy face and the truth I hadn't wanted to acknowledge to myself finally came out.

"He's a loser."

Dante's smile faded. I glanced down. When I looked back up, I saw another wave of disappointment cross his face. But it was true. Blake was using me. For my body or my money. Or both. I don't know why I hadn't seen it before. The knowledge stung, but I felt a wave of gratitude that I hadn't fallen for him. I'd fallen for guys in the past only to realize they were more interested in driving my Ferrari than getting to know who I really was.

Dante cupped my chin. I could barely meet his eyes. "Gia, you are better than that."

Was I? I didn't know anymore. I wondered if my poor batting average in love was because my expectations were unrealistically high. I grew up watching my parents' seemingly unearthly love for each other grow stronger every year. It made me feel hopeless at ever finding a love like that. Then, when I lost my parents I decided it hurt too much to give a shit about anyone or anything.

The older I got, the more I believed that I was fucked when it came to having any type of real, intimate relationship. Falling head over heels with my gay best friend in high school was just the beginning of my losing streak with love.

Dante stood watching me, waiting. I picked up my cell phone and sent a quick text. Dante raised one groomed eyebrow.

"Just canceled my date," I said and was rewarded with a big smile. We headed back to the restaurant.

The shadows had grown long by the time I finally got up to leave. As I drove away, I looked in my rearview mirror. Dante stood in the middle of the driveway with his hands on his hips. I kept glancing at his silhouette. He never moved. Finally, when he was a small black dot, I stopped looking.

CHAPTER SEVEN

THE NEXT AFTERNOON, I was sitting with my feet up on my balcony trying to decide where to go for lunch when my cell rang. I didn't recognize the number.

"This is Bobby. There's no easy way to say this. Christopher is dead."

I couldn't get enough air. My heart was racing and my lungs felt like they'd turned into sandbags. I stood, knocking my chair upside down, and walked like a zombie in circles around my apartment until I came to a stop in the dining room staring at my pale face in the mirrored wall.

Bobby's voice had been talking to me through the phone, but it had seemed to come from far away. I finally focused on his words. "Gia? You there? Gia?"

"Yes." My voice sounded foreign to me.

"I'm so sorry to be the one to tell you, Gia," Bobby said. He sounded out of breath. Making this call probably hadn't been easy for him.

Get it together, Gia.

"No, no, thank you for calling me," I said. His words had not quite sunk in. My brother. Dead. It couldn't be possible. I sank to the floor, holding the phone up against my ear so tightly it hurt. I was surprised to feel nothing. I didn't want to cry. I didn't want to scream. But I also wasn't sure I could move.

"Gia?"

"I'm here."

"What's your address? I'm coming over."

"I don't think that's a good idea."

"Give me your address." His voice was firm.

I recited my address robotically.

"Okay. Why don't you stay on the phone with me? I'm already in my car. I'll be there in two hours."

Oh shit. I'd just given him my address. He was serious.

"You can't come here."

"I'm coming if you like it or not. The question is whether you want me to stay on the phone with you the entire time."

I didn't answer. I had my face in my hands and was leaning against the mirrored wall in my dining room, staring into space.

"Gia?"

"How?"

"Huh?"

"How did Christopher die?"

"O.D.'d. He had a tourniquet and the needle was still in his arm." I heard him gulp for breath. "I found him in the bathroom. I called 911 and tried CPR ... but it was too late."

"What?" None of it was making sense. I was still stuck on the first words Bobby uttered: *Christopher is dead.* The words were running through my mind on a loop, faster and faster until the phrase blended into one. *Christopherisdead. Christopherisdead. Christopherisdead. Christopherisdead.*

"Yeah. It was probably some bad stuff."

Bobby's voice sounded like it was coming from far away. The side of my head was pressed tightly against the mirrored wall, which felt cool and soothing so I pressed harder until my head hurt. From the corner of my eye I stared at myself in the mirrored wall. I looked deranged.

Bobby kept speaking, but I was lost in memories of Christopher as his voice wobbled in and out, growing softer than louder.

One of my earliest memories involved my younger brother. It was the day I realized he was different from other people. I was five years old and Christopher was four—we were only fifteen months apart. Our nanny had taken us that day to Bubba Gump's for lunch. My mother, a full-blooded Sicilian, who took immense pride in her cooking, had forbidden we eat there. In my mother's opinion, Bubba Gump was the fast food restaurant of Monterey. Not to mention, my father's business imported seafood to the finest restaurants in Carmel. That's probably why we begged the new nanny to take us, knowing she didn't know any better.

It was the first time I got to try greasy and fried squid and seafood dipped in gallons of catsup. And the first time, but not the last, I would be afraid of my brother. After lunch, we all went to the Monterey Bay Aquarium. At one point, Christopher wandered off, sending the nanny into hysterics.

It was a few minutes after we left the tiny manta ray petting pool. Neither one of us had wanted to leave. The gentle creatures seemed to love the attention, poking their heads above water and letting kids stroke their velvety backs.

But the nanny had steered us to the giant tank with the tuna fish bigger than my bed. A few minutes passed before a commotion rose around the corner. That's when the nanny realized that Christopher was missing. The color drained from her face. She grabbed my hand and dragged me toward the noise. It was Christopher.

He'd caught a tiny manta ray by the tail and was bashing it against a concrete pole. Blood was splattering everywhere. Children were crying and parents were swooping them up and rushing out of the room. We got there just in time to see a white-faced aquarium worker grab Christopher from behind.

After thirty minutes of the nanny crying outside the security office, my godfather arrived, grim-faced and entered the room. A few minutes later he came out with Christopher and we all headed home.

The nanny and my godfather didn't tell my mother. I didn't either.

"Gia? You still there?"

I nodded, then realized he couldn't see me. "Where is he now?"

"His body?"

I nodded yes, but feeling my head move against the mirror, realized he couldn't see me. "Yes. Where did they take him?"

"I don't know." He cleared his throat. "I'll find out for you, though."

It didn't matter. I don't even know why I'd asked. "No, no that's okay."

I hung up without saying goodbye.

CHAPTER EIGHT

IT TOOK A WHILE BEFORE I understood that the sound I heard was someone pounding on my front door. I dragged myself away from the mirror and over to the peephole. My foot and one leg were both tingly and numb from falling asleep so I more hobbled than walked.

It was Bobby. I unlocked the door and turned, crossing the room to my bedroom where I plopped face down on my bed.

Then, Bobby's hand was on my hair, smoothing it down. It was what finally brought me to tears. I didn't look up, but shook, sobbing until not only my pillow, but the mattress around it was wet. I don't know how long I cried, but when I was finally done, I sat up. Bobby handed me a wad of toilet paper and I loudly blew my nose.

"Thanks."

"I'm sorry, Gia." He was dressed in faded jeans and a soft worn T-shirt. He smelled so good that I buried my face in his chest for a few seconds. There was something there, nagging at me, something just below the surface, as if I had forgotten something important. I didn't know what it was. I sniffled and pulled back from Bobby.

"I always thought it would be a relief to have Christopher out of my life. I never thought I would cry over him. I never liked him. I loved him, but didn't like him. My dad always told me that was okay—that you had to love everyone, but didn't have to like them or how they acted."

Bobby patted my back. As I sat there, I realized that maybe the truth was that I was grieving for all of them—my mother and father and Christopher. Christopher had been the only one who understood what it felt like to lose our parents. He was my last connection—the only one who could truly understand my loss.

Bobby didn't try to talk, which I appreciated. Instead, he looked at me intensely and listened, nodding.

"It sounds horrible to say," I went on, "but in a way, I'm glad my mother died first because Christopher's death would have been unbearable to her. She loved him despite who and what he was."

He was her favorite. I never understood it. When I was little I tried to make her eyes light up the way they did when she looked at him, but it was never the same. She would laugh at the silly things he did and when I did the exact same things, she would barely smile. I could never compete with him. Finally, I just grew to accept it and turned to my dad for the love I wanted. And my dad loved me as much as any little girl ever was loved by her father, but it still never took away the pain I had realizing my mother would never love me like she loved Christopher.

I told Bobby all of this.

Finally, after it grew dark he let go of my hand and headed toward my galley kitchen.

"Have you had anything to eat?" He poked his head around the corner.

I shook my head.

"Are you hungry?"

I shook my head again.

"Jesus," he said from the kitchen. "Don't you have any food in this house? I thought you were Italian."

"What the hell does that mean?"

Silence.

"I bet you were shocked that I wasn't making pasta by hand and listening to opera when you arrived. And oh, yeah, I forgot, my Virgin Mary statue is out on the balcony in case you missed it."

My voice caught on a sob. I closed my eyes.

Bobby was at my side on the couch, holding me.

"I'm sorry. I didn't mean to stereotype. I'm a buffoon."

"It's not that."

"I know," he said softly.

And then I said it, even though it made me sound like a monster. "What hurts the most is that my mother loved Christopher more than me and he was a sociopath. He didn't deserve a love like hers. He didn't deserve to be loved more than me."

There it was. Out in the open — the wound that would never heal.

Bobby didn't say anything, just held me.

Finally, my body stopped quaking. As I drifted off to sleep, a memory flooded back to me.

When Christopher lived in Argentina, he usually came home for Christmas. He spent most of the time in his room with headphones on listening to death metal.

He ignored me unless he was trying to bum money. Then he would lay on the charm thickly, the persona that he usually reserved for other girls. I knew he hated me and yet he made me feel like I was the coolest, most beautiful sister in the world. I realized then how dangerous he was.

One Christmas, at the last minute, my father was called away to business in Switzerland. My mother decided to rent a cabin on the snowy banks of Lake Tahoe. It was going to be a "field trip." When we were little and our father traveled, my mother often took us on educational "field trips." We would visit the Redwood Forest or go whale watching in Baja California or hot air ballooning in the Southwest. My mother's sense of adventure was always infectious. But the field trips had stopped when Christopher was sent to boarding camp.

That Christmas Eve in our small cabin at Tahoe we were on top of one another. A snowstorm most of the day kept us indoors. But around ten, the snow stopped and the skies cleared. My mother and brother were reading so I decided to go exploring down by the lake. The full moon lit up the area and made the snowy landscape seem magical. My mother made a worried face but I told her I'd be fine. Christopher didn't look up from his book.

The lakeshore was magical. Everything sparkled in the moonlight.

It was cold enough for my breath to puff out in front of me, but I was dressed warmly with my down coat, thick scarf, hat and mittens.

I ventured out onto the dock that normally held ski and fishing boats. There was a bench at the end and I wanted to sit there and gaze at the beauty around me.

About halfway to the bench, the wood of the deck gave out and I plunged into icy cold water, going completely under. My clothes were instantly waterlogged and my vision nothing but black. I struggled to break the surface but when I came up my head smacked into the bottom wooden dock. Dazed and panicking, I flailed, running out of breath, desperate for air and light.

I knew distantly that the dock wasn't that big that if I moved around some I would be sure to come out from under it, but the blow to the head had disoriented me. My limbs began to feel heavy and I felt myself slowly sinking until my feet touched something slimy.

At that moment, I was yanked hard and the next thing I know Christopher had flung me onto the dock. I was coughing and choking but breathing. I snuck a look at him, he was leaning over coughing and soaking wet, too.

He looked over at me and I saw something there I'd never seen before. Terror.

My brother had been worried about me. Frightened. For a brief second, I could've sworn he actually cared about me. Maybe even loved me. But then he turned his back and was gone, off the dock and up the hill to the cabin, not even waiting to see if I was behind him.

I got up and stumbled behind him. A few seconds later, my mother had flung open the door and ran to me, helping me up the hill. She put me in a warm bath and then to bed under a heap of old smelly quilts.

Christopher stayed in his room the rest of the night. In the morning, his car was gone. He'd already headed back to the Monterey Peninsula. When we got back the next day, he'd left a note from my mother saying he'd returned to Argentina early.

The next time I saw him he had come home for our parent's funeral.

He left right after the mass.

A week later, I followed suit, packing up and moving to San Francisco.

I WOKE ALONE THE NEXT morning on the couch, my neck stiff, smelling like something had died. I dragged myself into the shower. Bobby had left a note saying something about hitting Starbucks because he didn't really feel like drinking the beer in my frig for breakfast. He put a little smiley face by his name.

After my shower, I tugged on some yoga pants, a soft T-shirt and wrapped an old, warm cashmere sweater around me. I felt like I needed my blankie with me in the world today. I didn't bother with makeup. Nothing could disguise the circles under my eyes on this day.

When Bobby returned with almond croissants and lattes, he also had the *Chronicle* with him. We sat at my little café table on my balcony overlooking the Bay, munching, drinking coffee, and reading the paper. We didn't talk much. I had talked enough the night before for a lifetime. I kept sneaking glances at Bobby. His brow furrowed as he concentrated on what he was reading. It was cute. And too comfortable. Too normal having him there. I'd have to make an excuse for him to go.

CHAPTER NINE

BOBBY FINALLY LEFT. He looked like a puppy that got kicked when I told him I didn't think we should ever see each other again. Then he got mad, grabbed a permanent marker off my counter and wrote his phone number on my mirrored dining room wall. I gaped at it, only distantly hearing the front door slam shut. After a few stunned seconds of silence, I angrily scrubbed the mirror with glass cleaner. But not before I remembered I had his number on my cell phone from when he called.

I felt bad about kicking Bobby out, but if I didn't stop this thing right now, the next thing I knew I'd find myself doing something ridiculous like asking him to move in or something.

I'd never felt so alone in the world.

Every single blood relative I had was dead. Even though Christopher was a horrible person, he was my flesh and blood. When you were Italian-American, that meant something. He was also my last tie to my mother. Now that was gone, too.

The only thing I had left of my mother was that damn box. I stared at it on my computer desk. It had obviously been special to my mother. She had millions of dollars in jewelry sitting on her dressers in houses across the world and yet she found this box so precious, so valuable, that she was compelled to hide it.

The box was the key to her heart. It showed what really mattered to her. My father and Christopher and hopefully, if I dug around in it more, I'd find something that was proof of her love for me.

Maybe it was time to read the love letters. I needed to know it was possible to love someone and have them love you back just as much. Even if I never experienced that in my own life so far, I needed to believe that it existed. I wanted to cling to that belief. I poured a glass of cabernet sauvignon, my mother's favorite, gulped most of it in one sip, took a big breath, and opened the lid of the hat box.

The letter I'd found on the floor of their house addressed to my mother was on top. I tore it open.

At first I couldn't understand what I was reading, but when the implications of the letter became clear, I didn't make it to the bathroom before I threw up.

It was a letter from the widow of the doctor who had performed my parents' autopsies. The Geneva doctor had killed himself last month and left a note saying he had been paid off to lie on dozens of autopsy reports. Including my parents.

My parents did not die in an accidental fire. They were murdered.

The official report said they had burned to death in their lakeside Geneva home. The fire and subsequent deaths were ruled accidental, caused by an electrical short.

In reality, according to this letter, they both had bullets through their foreheads. As I read the letter, the horror of losing both my parents came back so hard I couldn't breathe. It was bad enough believing they had died in an accident, but to have been deliberately killed? And by someone powerful — or at least rich — enough to cover it up.

Murdered.

My parents had been murdered.

And now my brother was dead.

As soon as these two pieces of information met, I knew what had been nagging at me the day before. It was how Christopher died. The *way* he died.

During Christopher's long, rambling letters to me about Bridget, he had said several times that he blamed Bridget's heroin addiction for ruining his life, and making him incapable of loving anyone ever again.

His hatred for the drug was so fierce, he said, he was considering spending his life going after the big dealers in the world and taking them out. He called heroin evil.

Bobby said Christopher died of a heroin overdose.

I knew that even if his madness made him turn to the one drug he blamed for ruining his life, he still would never have shot it up. Even if Christopher had wanted to die, if he had found some poetic justice in killing himself the way Bridget had, he wouldn't have shot up. He would have snorted or smoked it.

He would never stick a needle in himself.

Ever since he was a little boy he'd had an unholy fear of needles.

To me, this all added up to one thing:

Christopher was murdered.

Somebody was methodically killing my family. They had disguised it with a fire.

Slumped on the floor near my mirrored dining room wall in a sick daze, I watched myself in the mirror as I dry heaved. My eyes were bloodshot with little pink blood bursts that had appeared around my eyelids from the violent motion.

Why would someone kill my parents? I had no idea. Christopher? Well there were a million reasons. But I was convinced all three deaths were related. But why? It wasn't for our family's money. If I died, the money would go to charity. My parents had stipulated that in their will. If Christopher and I died before we had children, any money at our deaths would go to the Make-A-Wish Foundation.

None of it made sense.

I sat staring at the wall with my hand pressed to my mouth for a good hour before I finally, wearily, dragged myself to bed where I stared at the ceiling for the rest of the night.

CHAPTER TEN

THE NEXT DAY, I DID everything I could to avoid thinking about the contents of the letter — or my realization that my entire family had been murdered. I sprawled on the couch in my pajamas. At times, I napped to make up for the previous sleepless night. Other times, I tuned into old black and white movies on the American classics station. I did everything to avoid thinking. But I knew I'd have to show the letter to my godfather. I'd head down to Carmel the next day.

I wondered if he already knew about Christopher's death. If so, I was sure he was relieved.

It was the information in the letter I was really worried about. The revelation that my parents had been murdered would be devastating to him. He was my parents' oldest and dearest friend. They had all grown up together in the same small Sicilian town. News that they were murdered might trigger a stroke or heart attack. I'd definitely have to warn his nurse before I let him read the letter.

By nighttime, I was restless. I ripped open my closet and threw all my clothes onto my bed. Finally, I settled on my favorite outfit, my super soft and worn-in leather pants, an oversized white T-shirt and a black blazer. I tugged on some Beatles-style flat boots and grabbed my apartment keys. I needed to get out of my place. So many things were racing through my mind I couldn't sit still. A few drinks would quiet my mind.

The second I walked in the door of Anarchy, the bartender, Scott, caught my eye and nodded so that by the time I made it through the Saturday late night crowd, he'd run off the college kids in my regular spot and had a tumbler of Patron waiting. I downed the clear amber liquid, savoring the tingling warmth in my throat and pushed the glass back toward him without saying hello.

He didn't raise an eyebrow, just refilled my glass.

I didn't bring up my tiff with him last week for cutting me off. Four hours later, he was wiping down the bar when he nudged my head. My cheek was sticking to something gooey on the smooth wood.

"Gia? You want me call a cab?"

I grumbled and a few minutes later Scott had his hands under both my arms and was carrying me out to the sidewalk and depositing me in a cab.

"10 Jones Street," Scott said and slammed the cab door shut.

"For Christ's sake, she can't walk two blocks?"

"Fuck offfff." I hollered from the backseat. They ignored me. But Scott must have handed the cabbie some cash because the car lurched forward. I think I dozed off for a second because the next thing I knew my doorman had lifted me from the cab and dumped me in the elevator.

Pushing him away, I said, "I'm fine. Just sleepy."

Before he closed the door, he rummaged around in my bag and put my house key in my palm. I threw it on the elevator floor.

"Ms. Santella, this elevator comes back down here with you in it, I won't have a choice, I'll have to call your godfather . . ."

"Oh, fuck it. I'm fine, God damn it." My words were slurred, but I didn't care. So, what? Was it suddenly against the law to tie one on? My godfather paid for my place out of the trust, but that didn't mean he was in charge of me. I was twenty-three-years old for Christ's sakes.

Lying in my bed a few minutes later with the room spinning, I wasn't fine. I was fucked up. Again. At least this time I didn't have some stranger in bed with me.

I drifted off to thoughts of my mother and father in bed with bullet holes through their foreheads. The nightmares grew in intensity until I woke with fright. Something was in my room.

Two shapes at the foot of my bed stood right near where the bright moonlight stretched in from the long wall of window.

My eyes were slits while I surreptitiously curled my hand near my head. It came back with my gun aimed at one guy's crotch. I raised myself slowly to my knees and without looking, clicked on my bedside lap. Seeing the gun, the man closest to my bed put up his hands.

"Tell your buddy to toss his gun over here," I said.

"Easy, now," said one guy, dressed in designer slacks and a silk shirt. He looked like he'd been stuck on the 1970s train for a few years. He put out his hand in defense as if that would stop a bullet. The other guy near my dresser, wearing black jeans and a tight black T-shirt, must have been the muscle. He gave me the stink eye.

"Do it!" My voice was hoarse. I remembered then that I'd bummed half a dozen cigarettes off the guy at the bar beside me.

"Okay, okay," the 70s-guy nodded. The muscle shrugged, pulled a heavy looking gun out of his holster and tossed it on the floor by the bathroom door with a heavy thud. Still closer to him than me. Shit.

"Yours too."

The 70s-guy sighed and pulled a smaller gun out of his waistband, tossing it onto the bed, "We're just here to talk."

I didn't want to talk.

I aimed to the left of the 70s-guy's crotch and released the safety. The guy jumped about a foot. "Easy now," he said again. "We tried knocking."

"Get the fuck out of my place. Now." My hand was shaking, from adrenaline, fear, and the weight of the gun, but my voice was steel. I was naked but I leaped out of my covers and onto my bed, standing with the gun held in both hands before me.

"Look at my tits and you die."

The men both held their hands up and raised their eyes. "Jesus H. Christ. We just got a message. From your godfather." The 70s-man's voice was even.

My godfather? I lowered the gun. The 70s-man started walking my way.

"He wants you to come back with us. To his house."

"In the middle of the fucking night? Are you crazy?" I held the gun back up.

"Like I said, I don't ask questions of Mr. Guidi."

That made sense. Maybe my godfather heard about Christopher's death and sent these two goons to escort me safely to Monterey.

That's when I saw something behind the muscle. On top of my dresser, beside my perfume bottles, lay a pair of black gloves, a coil of rope, and a duffel bag with a black plastic roll sticking out of it.

They weren't here to talk.

My face grew warm. That's when I knew.

The warrior knows that there are times in life when we must fight to the death. When every day becomes a battle. When we lose all faith in everything we've known, in everyone we've known, when our closest allies have become our enemies. When we realize that if we must die, we will go down fighting: ripping, kicking, biting, scratching, tearing and punching. We fight to the last breath and never ever give in or give up.

Someone wanted me dead, too. My own godfather. My knees grew weak. In an attempt to disguise it, I kneeled down onto my bed. Keeping my eyes on the men I reached behind me, under my pillow. When I snapped the silencer on, the 70s-guy started hopping from foot to foot.

"We'll leave now."

"Fuck you." My intention had been to shoot them both in the legs and then run. But I thought better of it. I needed some things from my place first. Besides, they seemed to be paying a little bit more attention to me now that I'd put the silencer on the gun.

"I'm going to ask you to slowly turn around and walk out of my bedroom. I'm going to be right behind you. You're going to walk to my front door, walk down the hall to the elevator, get in and never come back. My gun has Teflon-coated slugs, you morons might know them as Cop Killers, so if either one of you monkey around, I'll shoot both of you through the back with one bullet. Got it?"

The 70s-guy nodded. The muscle guy looked bored.

I followed them, my entire body shaking, the weight of the gun almost unbearable. I waited until my front door clicked closed. I slid the deadbolt and stuck my eye to the peephole. It wasn't until their backs disappeared into the elevator that the full implication of what happened hit me. I slumped to the floor, holding my head in my hands. My own godfather, the one person left on earth I thought loved me, wanted me dead.

CHAPTER ELEVEN

I THREW A FEW PAIRS of jeans, a couple T-shirts, my laptop, my gun, ammo, the box from my mom, and all the cash in my safe — about forty thousand dollars — into a large camping backpack. I put on my jeans, boots, and a leather jacket, tugged a thick cotton stocking cap over my hair and peeked out my door. No sign of the goons. I hit the button for the elevator and then sprinted for the stairs. I left through the backdoor of the building, cutting through a nearby residential street down to Columbus Avenue and hailed a cab in front of a strip club. Within thirty minutes, I was in front of Kato's house.

Even though it was four in the morning, when he opened the door, Kato looked like he'd been waiting for me to arrive.

"I need help. I need a place to hide."

He didn't even blink.

"Come in. The coffee's hot."

It was that sixth sense he had. He didn't even comment on my appearance or the huge backpack I was lugging.

"My godfather wants me dead." I didn't elaborate and Kato didn't push. Every time my mind wandered in that direction, I thought of something else. A constant stomach pain since I'd left my place was the only indication that the revelation was affecting me.

Kato poured me a cup of coffee and handed me the newspaper while he showered. By the time he was done, the kids were up and acting bashful to find *Gia-Ko* in their kitchen.

"I have a place for you to hide," Kato said, handing me a weird green smoothie that smelled—and tasted, frankly—like dirt. "I just need to make a few calls. Give me an hour or two."

I hung out with Susie and the boys until Kato called from work and left a cryptic address. He told me the place wouldn't be ready until the next day. This worried me. The longer I stayed with Kato and his family, the more danger they might be in. My godfather was a very powerful man and had eyes everywhere.

Using their phone, I made a few calls, including to my friend, Darling, who could procure anything for anybody anytime. By afternoon, I'd snuck into the North Beach strip club, keeping a wary eye out for anyone who might be working for my godfather. Every time I thought about Vito, I pushed down the part of me that wanted to feel sorry for myself. There would be time for that later. I needed to be cold and clinical if I was going to outsmart my godfather.

My godfather was powerful, but he had a weakness I intended to exploit — he underestimated me. For instance, he probably thought I was still holed up in my luxury apartment, shaking from fear from his murder attempt. I had to use that to my advantage.

After I went over the plans with stripper girl Candy for the third time, I swung by a photo place and had some pictures taken. I paid extra for them to rush the order and then sent them by courier to my friend Darling's shop. Back at Kato's I called and finally reached Darling. She'd gotten the photos. Her connections would have fake ID's and passports for me by the next afternoon.

My plan was almost in place.

One more night.

The next morning I was up early. I packed my bag and said my goodbyes to Kato and his family, sticking the address he had given me in my pocket before I hailed a cab to take me to Russian Hill. I had one last stop before I headed to my new home.

CHAPTER TWELVE

I ADJUSTED THE BINOCULARS and watched the dark-haired woman walk into the driveway of my building. Candy was rocking my white Versace suit, my favorite gold Jimmy Choo stilettos, and giant dark sunglasses.

I'd told her to wait until my doorman had his usual smoke break. She followed directions good. And looked good doing it. I spotted one of my Hermes bags slung over her shoulder and my favorite Louis Vuitton suitcase on wheels behind her. *Sayonara,* baby. I wouldn't miss any of it. She tossed her hair and dipped her lithe body into the limo like she'd been riding in one her whole life. Perfect.

The warrior is always one step ahead of his enemies. While his enemies sleep and eat and drink, the warrior is making a battle plan.

The wind was icy on top of the neighbor's skyscraper rooftop, but I didn't lower my binoculars until the limousine pulled onto Columbus Avenue. Thanks, Candy. Have a nice stay in Cannes. I'd set her up to look like she was taking a red-eye to Costa Rica. But she'd only be in Central America for thirty minutes. She'd been instructed to use my cell phone heavily, calling and texting a list of numbers I'd given her, including texting my godfather once she landed in Costa Rica telling him she was sorry, but she needed some time alone after Christopher's death. Once she was in the Costa Rica airport, she was instructed to head immediately to a bathroom where she'd change into jeans and a blonde wig. She'd rip the SIM card out of the phone, flush it down the toilet and then smash the phone to bits before she took out a new passport and slipped onto another plane bound for the south of France.

If she followed my plan exactly, no one would be any wiser. And nobody would get hurt. She'd stay in the Cannes apartment I'd rented for the next year and then, if she wanted, she could fly back into America with the one-way ticket I'd bought her under her real name.

I'd spent last night at Kato's transferring important documents and information from my old laptop to one I'd paid cash for at a store on Market Street. I'd then put some vague, obscure posts on social media about craving warmth and sunshine and being sick of San Francisco's perpetually gloomy skies.

I should be the one using that passport and hiding out. At first, I'd considered fleeing to the south of France myself, but then I realized that is what would be expected of me. Staying in the city and living in the ghetto was the least likely place for me to hide. That's what I was counting on. Hiding in plain sight. And it would allow me to investigate who was trying to off me. Was it really Vito?

I paced a bit on the rooftop, keeping an eye on the wide curving driveway of my building — or rather my old building — until my godfather's men showed up. The black Lincoln Continental was not subtle. It squealed to a halt in the driveway. The goons didn't bother closing the car doors after they leaped out. The doorman rushed out of his office, hands up, mouth working. He ducked and I felt a little bad when the muscle slapped him on the side of his head, sending his coiffed hair askew. Not cool. But the doorman was obviously in on it. He'd let the goons up to my apartment the other night and now called my godfather's men to report "me" leaving. I wondered how long my godfather had been spying on me and how long the doorman had been at his service. Fuck me. I had to be smarter.

The 70s-dude paced the driveway, phone to his ear. His scowl was visible from fourteen stories up. I'm sure my godfather was chewing him a new asshole. Training the binoculars up to my sixteenth-floor balcony, I could see the muscle tearing apart my apartment, throwing cushions across the room. Satisfied, I put the binoculars away.

CHAPTER THIRTEEN

I STEPPED OFF THE BUS into the long shadows of the Tenderloin—the T.L.—as the sun set. Tourists staying at hotels near the Curran Theatre took cabs the three blocks to the theater to avoid stepping their dainty feet on these soiled city streets. They pulled their fur coats closer and darted glances at me and the other misfits roaming the area. I didn't blame them. It was good people watching in the T.L.

In the space of five blocks, I strolled past a dude dropping his drawers and crapping in the middle of the sidewalk, a pair of junkies passing a crack pipe back and forth, and a hooker in a skimpy skirt hailing a Mercedes and leaning in his window so far that her sex was showing.

I wasn't sure, but it seemed like a guy in a stocking cap might have been following me since I got off the bus so I backtracked to the Market Street bus stop and spent some extra time going up and down the escalators at Marshalls until I was sure I ditched him before I ducked into the Fancy Gurlz hair salon. Women with elaborate braids sat beneath pastel cone hairdryers. The salon reeked of hair straightener and cheap perfume and the ladies cackled at my appearance.

"You hanging with the sisters tonight?"

"What you want with your shiny brown hair?"

"You know the joint is slipping when they start letting white girls come in get their hair did."

I ignored them and kept walking toward the back. They hooted and hollered until Darling, the owner, whose gloved hands were buried in a woman's hair, spoke up. "Hush, now. Baby girl's a friend of mine."

I leaned over and gave Darling a kiss on her cheek and she jutted her chin back toward her office.

Darling and I had history. We met during a protest a few years back. A cop had killed a young black man who'd done nothing more than been in the wrong place at the wrong time when the trigger-happy rookie got scared and bam-o, dead kid.

Darling and I ended up in the back office of her shop after the protest, drinking bourbon and playing cribbage and trying to peacefully reform society. Soon, I learned that the salon was her love, her passion, but also a front. Her real money—the money that let her have a house on Russian Hill *and* in the Oakland Hills—was paperwork, the expensive and hard to get kind, such as fake IDs and passports.

Even without that, the salon was the epicenter of a vast social network I knew nothing about. Darling once told me that when World War III hit, the black people's hair salons would still be standing, doing fierce business. I believed her.

Today I looked homeless, lugging my giant camping backpack as I walked all the way through the salon to the office door. Inside the top drawer of her desk, there was an envelope marked "G" that contained the other fake IDs I'd asked for and a stash of burner cell phones. I left an envelope with two grand to pay for my and Candy's fake passports, ID's, the expense of having Candy's documents couriered to her, and of course for Darling's trouble. Tucking the envelope into my jacket pocket, I went out another door. This one led down a flight of stairs, across a hallway, through another door, and up another set of stairs that led to a back door to the alley. Out in the fresh air I got my bearings and hurried to the next block. Off the main drag, I turned into another long alley and from there onto a small, quiet street. I checked the address on the slip Kato had given me. Yep. There it was. 345 Turk Street, across from the Tenderloin hood known as Forgotten Island. I'd read about it in the paper a few years ago. Forgotten Island. That's what I wanted to be — forgotten, disappeared, invisible. That was a great reason to make this tiny strip of the T.L.— my new home.

A woman with ratty hair pulled back in a silky, stained scarf and a face caked with dirt and sweat scrambled up from the sidewalk in front of the building when I got to the stoop. She smiled, showing a few missing teeth.

"Spare some change?"

I stopped, my hand on the door. "You live here?"

Looking around at the empty sidewalk, she shrugged.

"What's your name?"

"My name?" For a minute her eyebrows met in the middle as she scrunched up her face. I got the feeling nobody had asked her that for a long time. "I'm Ethel. Ethel Swanson." Her shoulders seemed to draw back a little in pride when she said this.

"Well, Ethel. I'm Gia. Nice to meet you." I gave her a quick salute and opened the door to go in. Ethel scowled and sank back down onto the stack of cardboard on the sidewalk.

INSIDE THE BUILDING the bulb was burned out, but I was able to make my way by the dim streetlight shining through the glass front door. Something scuttled across the floor, but it was too dark to tell if it was a cockroach or a rat.

I pounded on the door to apartment A for about ten minutes.

"Who there?"

"I'm looking for Trang. Name's Gia."

The door creaked open a few inches and one squinting bloodshot eye peeked out. Strands of black hair stuck up in every direction.

"Okay, okay."

Trang undid the chain and gestured for me to enter, but I had no intention of leaving the hallway.

"You got the money?"

I handed him another envelope with three thousand dollars in it. He counted it carefully.

"What's up with the dark?"

He squinted up at the ceiling as if he had just noticed. "Damn. Burned out. I fix."

I gave him a skeptical look. What kind of dump was I moving into?

He started to close the door. "Okay, come back in one hour."

"What the fuck are you talking about?"

"I don't have the key here. I gotta go get it." He pulled on an Army green coat and locked his door behind him. "Meet me back here in an hour."

"What?" he asked when I didn't answer. "You want receipt?"

I turned to walk away. The piece of paper would've been useless.

Outside the building, that same woman, Ethel, sat huddled on the ground. She started to get up, saw it was me again, and slumped back down.

"Hey Ethel, why so glum?" I pulled a silver flask out of my bag. It was engraved with my initials G.V.S.—for Giada Valentina Santella. I took a slug and handed it to her.

She grasped it eagerly with dirty fingernails and tipped it back, gulping, her eyes on mine. I nodded and she kept going, finally coming up for air. She got up to hand it to me, but I waved her off.

"All yours." The flask had been a twenty-first birthday present from my godfather and I'd gotten a good two years use out of it, but I wouldn't need it anymore. Before I got up to hunt down more booze, I tucked a twenty into the pocket of her jacket and told her to go buy herself dinner.

CHAPTER FOURTEEN

I SPENT AN HOUR DRINKING tequila at the closest bar, which was actually only a block away from my new home. I'd heard the Beastie Boys coming out of the juke box when I walked in and figured it was a cool place to hang out for a while.

The crowd at Club Katrina looked okay — pretty typical San Francisco dive bar crowd — a transvestite or two, a grizzly old guy, and a couple of working ladies. Nobody who seemed dangerous. Two rowdy yuppie-looking guys came in right behind me, obviously slumming because they were talking loudly about the show they were about to attend at the Great American Music Hall a few blocks away.

I ordered another Patron tequila from the surprisingly beautiful Asian bartender, who could have obviously found a gig at a better place. I slumped into a sticky booth and sat idly watching the ten o'clock news on the TV hanging above the bar. The lead story was about the opening of the new span of the Bay Bridge. Boring.

I grabbed the *Chronicle* off a nearby table and settled in to read.

Two articles in the local section nearly made me fall off my bar stool.

The first was a picture of the girl I'd seen with Christopher. The article said she was missing and her parents were frantic. My heart pounded in my ears. Holy fuck. Had my brother been killing girls? Is that why Vito was so serious about stopping him. Had Vito killed him to stop him from killing others? That made sense. But then why would Vito want me dead? Because I knew?

It hurt too much to think about. I had loved Vito. But my love was growing into hatred.

Christopher had probably killed that girl. And maybe, although it was hard to believe, Vito had killed him and tried to kill me.

Staring at the girl's face, I felt a wave of horror.

I had failed. It was my job to protect her. I knew that night I saw her with Christopher that she was in danger. I ignored my Budo training and walked away. I had thrown her to the wolves, or the biggest, baddest wolf: my brother.

I rushed to the bathroom and had barely made it to the toilet when I vomited. I could have saved that girl. I could have taken her aside and done ... something. Lied or something. Anything to get her away from my brother. And what the fuck? Did Bobby know this? I let that guy in my apartment and in my bed. What if they were in on it together? But I knew that was nonsense. Bobby must not know.

Finally, when there was no more tequila in me, I splashed my face and fixed my hair and went back to the bar to order another.

The ethereally beautiful bartender gave me a skeptical look when I ordered another drink. The newspaper was still on the bar, open to the girl's picture.

I stared at it.

I flipped the page so I didn't have to see her anymore. Her blood was practically on my own hands.

I read about a new organics recycling program and a new book out about the Mission. Then, a small item caught my eye. A doorman for a luxurious apartment building, named Andrew Fairfield, had been killed in a car crash. As I read, my blood raced, Fairfield had decided to go joyriding in a tenant's red Ferrari. He'd taken the car across the Golden Gate Bridge and just reached the Marin Headlands and was navigating a tricky curve when the car went plunging off the road and hurtling down a cliff. He died on impact. Police were investigating, but said it appeared that the brake line had been cut.

Andrew Fairfield. My doorman. Red Ferrari. My car.

Whoever wanted me dead wasn't taking any chances. They were serious about taking me out. Vito was ruthless. I knew this. But what had I done? It didn't make sense.

I paid my bill and headed back to my new home, looking behind me at every tiny noise. Back at 345 Turk Street, the lightbulb in the lobby was fixed. The place didn't look all that bad. Trang was waiting. He handed me the key and pointed up. "One at the top."

I made my way up the stairs until they ended at a small hallway where there was a reinforced steel door with a peephole. My key fit.

Kato had told me the apartment had been remodeled as a safe house for some political friend of his from Sudan. I didn't ask for more information and he didn't volunteer any.

I pushed open the door and hit the light switch. The apartment was about 800-square-feet of wooden-floored, wide-open space. The southwest corner had a single bed under a window. Across from that, on the northwest wall, was a small galley kitchen and café table with two chairs near another window. I took my mother's box and slid it on top of the highest cupboard in the small galley kitchen. A door opened to a small staircase leading to a door with a small sign that said "roof."

As I took in the wide-open space I rejoiced. It would be perfect to practice my Budo because I intended to get in the best shape of my life.

I'd go cold turkey on the alcohol and weed. I'd detox. I needed all my wits about me. There was no room for vices. I would need to prepare both my mind and body for the days ahead. I needed to be sharp as hell if I was going to find out whether my godfather killed my mom and dad. And Christopher. And why he wanted me dead.

That first night in the big, empty apartment, I couldn't sleep. I lay in the tiny hard twin bed staring at the ceiling for what seemed like hours, watching the lights flicker across my ceiling as cars drove by. Finally, I went up on the roof and paced, looking at the city around me, wishing I had a cigarette.

Finally, around dawn, I fell asleep.

Day blended into day and slowly the cravings for nicotine, booze, and weed went away. It helped that I was focusing on Budo more than ever, spending a few hours a day training. When I wasn't training, I was reading one of the books out of a giant stack that Kato and Susie had loaned me. Books on karate, but also ones by some of the San Francisco beat writers, such as Carolyn Cassady's book about her love affairs with Neal Cassady and Jack Kerouac.

It'd only been a week and I already missed Kato and my *dojo*. But that is the first place my godfather would go looking if he suspected I was still in town. I knew even if my godfather tracked down Kato's home address, none of his neighbors in the rough Mission District would talk to my godfather's men. Even if a gun was held to their face.

On the seventh day, I started doing pushups in the mornings and ran laps on the roof at night. I was relieved that whoever designed this safe house made it so my apartment was the only one with roof access. I was antsy holed up in my place, so I spent a lot of time up there, peering over the five-foot high walls at the streets below. So far, I hadn't seen anyone suspicious.

On the rare days when the sun graced the city, I brought an old blanket up to the roof to lie on and stripped naked, soaking up the warmth, pretending I was in the southern France penthouse where I'd sent Candy. I idly dreamed of one day growing tomatoes and basil on the roof so I could make fresh pasta sauce. Until then, I ate simply, eating a mixture of beans and brown rice or heating up some pasta and mixing it with butter and garlic salt, an old recipe my mother had showed me, saying she made it during the lean years of my childhood — before my dad's seafood business hit gold.

It felt good to detox. I'd been overindulging in everything in my life — food, alcohol and sex — since my parents died.

Cutting all that out made me feel more like myself than I'd felt in years.

One day, I went down to ask Trang something, but he wasn't home. My Vietnamese neighbors were quiet. The whole building smelled like their cooking, night and day, and made my mouth water. They kept to themselves. And so did I.

But on this day, as I stood near the glass front door, I saw one of my neighbors for the first time. An older woman juggled several grocery bags as she fumbled for her keys, trying to get the door open. One bag broke and oranges started rolling down the steps. I opened the door and picked up her scattered groceries, giving a quick glance around. Nobody. Not even Ethel.

Inside the building, the old Vietnamese lady gave me a missing tooth grin and said something I didn't understand. I followed her up the stairs to the second floor, holding her broken sack and four oranges close to my chest. She unlocked her door and turned to get her groceries from me, giving me a pat on the shoulder and another grin. She said something else in Vietnamese. I started to back away.

"Uh, okay. Yeah, you're welcome."

She just kept smiling and nodding as I headed up the stairs.

CHAPTER FIFTEEN

I WAS DOING MY BUDO the next morning when a knock at my door sent me scrambling for my gun. I raced to the side of the reinforced steel door, heart pounding, gun in hand, and yelled in what I hoped was a tough voice, "Who's there?"

Nothing. I stepped over to the peephole.

It was the little old lady from the second floor with a plate of steaming egg rolls. When I opened the door, she thrust the food at me, patting my arm and smiling. Before I could say a word, she had turned and skittered down the stairs. I wolfed all eight of the egg rolls down within minutes. I couldn't remember when anything had tasted so good.

After I'd been living in the T.L. for nearly three weeks, I woke up one morning and realized that I'd nearly run out of the massive amounts of food that had been stocked in the cupboards.

I pulled my hair back in a baseball cap, dressed in baggy clothes and sneakers and headed out. It was my lazy man's disguise. Like I said, nobody in his or her right mind would ever think the Italian Princess would go slumming in the Tenderloin. Not the girl who'd drop thousands of dollars at Saks Fifth Avenue during the day and spend her nights guzzling top-shelf booze at the finest bars in town.

Despite this, I felt right at home with the kind of people who lived in the T.L. The funny part is that only the tourists think the Tenderloin is the most dangerous part of the city. Any San Francisco cop will tell you it's Hunter's Point. I heard that in the 90s, city bus drivers had police escorts when they ventured into that neighborhood. I don't know if it's true or not. If you had any street smarts whatsoever, the T.L. wasn't all that bad.

On this day, strolling through the Tenderloin square with a canvas tote bag full of food, groups of winos huddled, eyeing me as they took long pulls off bottles peeking out of paper bags. The homeless men blended into one gray-brown mass of dingy, ill-fitting clothes. But one guy stood out. He was a skinny crankster with pockmarked pale skin and crazed eyes wearing an oversized Army jacket. He was trying to get an emaciated dog to stop eating out of a fast food bag.

"I tole you to knock that shit off," he said and grabbed the dog's muzzle and shook it. The dog whimpered in pain. When the man let go, the dog tried to run away, the whites of its eyes looking back frightened at the man. The man jerked violently on the rope tied to the dog's collar, dragging the dog on its side back to him.

I kept walking.

The warrior does not walk around life looking for battle or an excuse to demonstrate strength or superiority. The warrior knows that there is a fine line between being a warrior and being a bully.

Then the man kicked the dog in the side, making the animal howl in pain.

The warrior stands up for those who are weak, for the innocent, for the vulnerable.

I stopped a few feet away. Without turning around, I closed my eyes and said, "Leave the dog alone."

"What did you say, bitch?"

I turned around and met the man's eyes. "Leave the dog alone."

"What? Like this?" He aimed his boot at the dog's head. Before the kick connected, I had the man on the ground, my forearm against his neck, pushing down until he was sputtering for breath. I stared at him and he glared back. There was not a glimmer of humanity in those eyes.

Before I got up, I unwrapped the rope from around his arm and gathered the dog up against my chest. It must have weighed forty pounds, but I stood above the man, holding the dog, my tote bag, and watching as he clutched at his throat, gasping for air.

"You don't deserve this dog. You barely deserve to be alive."

BACK IN MY APARTMENT, I wadded up a blanket on the floor near my bed and gently laid the dog on it. It was some type of mutt that looked like it was part lab and maybe pit bull. I got out my first aid kit and dabbed some antiseptic ointment on some of the more obvious cuts. The dog shivered and licked at its wounds, the whites of its eyes looking up at me gratefully.

I opened up a can of chili and poured it in a bowl. The dog greedily gulped it up and looked at me for more. By ransacking my new groceries, I managed to add some tuna fish to the bounty. The dog also gulped that down. Later, I'd tackle giving it a bath.

The dog was awfully cute, but a small feeling of regret crept into me. I didn't want the responsibility of taking care of something else. I'd proven how irresponsible I was even keeping a plant alive at my old place. That's one reason I'd never had a dog or other pet before. I didn't want some other living thing to be dependent on me. I had a hard-enough time taking care of myself and I definitely didn't like having anything around that needed something from me. And pets had needs. And schedules. They needed to eat and poop and be exercised. I didn't like having to be home at a certain time to feed or walk a pet. But now I guess I'd have to get used to it.

I made vegetable stir fry with my stash of fresh food and flipped through the paper. There it was. An obituary for Christopher. Three weeks after his death. I suppose my godfather had arranged it, which surprised me.

The obit said very little, mainly talking about my parents, but it did say Christopher's funeral was scheduled for later this week. It would be too dangerous to attend. My godfather would have all his henchmen on the lookout for me, I was sure. Maybe that's why he'd submitted the obit — maybe as a trap to lure me to Monterey. Well, it wasn't going to work.

But something in me wanted to say my own goodbye to my brother. Maybe for my mother's sake. I'd figure out a way to do so. I'd do it for her.

TWO DAYS BEFORE CHRISTOPHER'S funeral, I made my plans, getting the dog set up for my absence.

I'd decided to name him Django after he thumped his tail approvingly when I repeatedly played a Django Reinhardt song on my phone one night. I kept the door to the roof propped open and trained him to head up there to do his business. But I knew he needed to be walked. I'd start doing that as soon as I got back from Monterey.

I piled a large dish with food and set about eight giant bowls full of water in case he knocked a few over and left the lid to the toilet open just in case that didn't work. I'd only be in Monterey for the day. I knew he'd be fine. He was like me—a survivor.

CHAPTER SIXTEEN

THE MAN AT THE RENTAL car agency didn't blink when I paid cash and handed over an I.D. saying my name was Nancy Johnson. He walked me through the inspection of the low-profile four-door sedan quickly because I told him I was running late. I'd dressed like a businesswoman in slacks and a white blouse with sensible shoes I'd bought at Marshall's on the way there, changing in the store's bathroom. My hair was in a bun and I had big Elvis Costello-style black glasses and little pearl studs in my ears.

I yacked about this laser eye surgery convention I was attending in Monterey that weekend and how excited I was. I knew it was overkill. But my plan was to operate as if I were a fugitive from the law. Anything less could mean my godfather and his wide web of cronies would be on to me. I knew my godfather well enough to suspect he was devoting all his manpower to finding me. Hopefully they were all looking in Costa Rica.

I parked the rental car a few blocks away and walked toward the water. It was the perfect time to find my godfather starting his regular Saturday morning bocce ball game near Fisherman's Wharf. He didn't play anymore, just sat in his wheelchair and exchanged friendly insults with his friends.

This morning, the crowds in the Custom House Plaza square near the bocce courts were fierce, shoulder-to-shoulder. When I was growing up, I remember hearing that the population on the Monterey

Peninsula doubled on weekends from all the tourists. In my family, that meant we stuck to our Pebble Beach compound on the weekends, saving our outings for midweek. But today I welcomed the crowds as I blended into them. Even better, today the artichoke festival was going on in the square adjacent to the bocce courts.

Live bands, bouncy houses for kids, food booths. I stopped to buy a churro, looking over at the courts. There was my godfather, smoking a cigar and joshing with his old Italian buddies. His nurse was sitting nearby. The game hadn't started yet. Once it had, I knew my godfather wouldn't be back to his home for at least two hours. After the game, the old timers always went to have lunch and drinks at nearby Jack's restaurant in the Portola Hotel.

That was the real relaxation period. The men would drink wine and eat oysters or pasta with scallops. The game itself was actually business disguised as pleasure. Multi-million-dollar business deals were made on that court. The Sicilians in Monterey had a code of honor that didn't require a handshake. Men knew better than to break any deal brokered on the bocce ball courts. Not if they wanted their families to stay safe.

It made me wonder if my parents' death was a hit, a contract murder, that my godfather had arranged. Not that the thought hadn't crossed my mind before. The only reason I didn't jump on that theory right away is that usually mob hits are obvious — the gangsters I knew left calling cards, like cutting someone's tongue out who had talked too much. Part of the power of the mob was the fear they could instill in the toughest man, so a hit without a calling card would be considered a waste of time.

I ordered an Americano from a coffee stand and planted myself at a café table between some buildings with a great view of the bocce courts. A wave of sadness washed over me as I watched my godfather laughing with his friends. I pushed the sorrow down into a dark hidden place inside. I had no time to love someone who didn't love me. There was no room for any more sadness in my heart. My grief, my sorrow, was reserved exclusively for my parents who loved me until the day they died.

I watched and waited for about fifteen minutes and then figured it was safe to leave.

I PARKED ON THE NEXT street over from my godfather's Carmel house and climbed the fence into the backyard. When I was little, I'd often stayed overnight in the back bedroom. Then, when I was a teenager, I would stay at my godfather's when my parents were out of the country. One night, I'd jerry-rigged the window so I could sneak out and meet a bunch of friends heading to a bonfire in Big Sur. That became my routine when I was a teen staying with Vito. I figured he never knew about it and therefore, had never fixed the window. I was right.

I removed the nail from the jamb and slid the window open. I got a grease spot on my slacks clambering inside and smacked my elbow hard when I landed on the floor. The bedroom was still decorated in the pink and greens my godfather had arranged for me when I was little. His office was only a few feet away.

In his office, the giant wooden desk took up the entire center of the room. It was made from an old door, a remnant of the days before he had money. My godfather once told me it helped him remember where he came from. But the rest of the room was sumptuous with Tiffany lamps, plush leather furniture and walls lined with bookshelves full of first editions.

His desktop computer was impregnable. I half-heartedly tried a few random passwords. It wasn't the first time in my life I wished I was a hacker. After a few minutes, I gave up on the computer and started rifling through the papers on top of his big desk. Boring. All business stuff for my father's seafood business.

There was one bill that seemed unusual. It was a late notice saying that payment had never been made to a supplier. The bill was for one hundred thousand. Something that wouldn't make a dent in the corporation's bank account. Was the company in financial trouble or was Vito's memory slipping?

I kept flipping through the papers. A thick folder was labeled BAY VIEW DEVELOPMENT. It contained information about some business deal up in San Francisco. So far, my father's seafood business dealings had stuck to the Monterey Peninsula. I skimmed it. From what I could piece together, my godfather was trying to develop a chunk of land in the Sunset district. Or rather, the seafood corporation, with its real estate arm, which Vito now had taken over, was proposing the development.

The Sunset District was bordered on the north by Golden Gate Park. Ocean Beach makes up its western border. From what I could glean, the company wanted to develop high-end, mixed-use condominiums in this location.

It sounded like the ground floor would be upscale shops, such as Tiffany & Co., Louis Vuitton, and Armani. The six floors above would hold luxury, 2,500-square-foot condominiums with sweeping views of the ocean.

As I read on, it looked like the project had a major roadblock.

A woman owned a house smack dab in the middle of the proposed development and was refusing to sell. My father's company had bought up all the surrounding houses and already demolished them, leaving this woman and her house an island in the middle of a pile of dirt.

The development wouldn't happen if the property owner, a woman named Jessica Stark, refused to sell her home and land. It looked like someone had jumped the gun and bought everything before they had a deal with the most important property owner.

She obviously had a good reason to hold out, I thought as I flipped through the notes because Vito had offered her a million dollars for her tiny, 1950s home and she had refused.

I knew if my father were alive, he would have let it go. He would rather lose a million dollars than ruin someone's life. I flipped through papers looking at the dates. The first mention of the deal was when my father was alive. But somewhere along the way, the project had stalled. Probably when Stark refused to sell.

However, it looked like recently, new city permits were pulled and the project was going full bore again.

Something about this deal felt really wrong. For starters, my father would roll over in his grave that his company was trying to force Ms. Stark out of her home. He always said people and families came first.

But there was something else that rubbed me wrong. I stared at the paperwork trying to figure it out. Something just below the surface, a niggling thought, a memory I couldn't quite grasp, told me this was a bad deal, but I didn't know why. I'd sleep on it. I'd put my brain to work at night remembering just why this deal set off alarms in my head.

I put the papers back in order. I'd let my subconscious work on it.

My Budo training had taught me the value of this.

Honing combat skills is the path to perfecting the self and maintaining the ancestral spirit and mind of the warrior. Once trained, the mind of a warrior has the ability to recall everything through deep meditation that the physical body once experienced and viewed.

Next, I flipped through the file folders in his drawers. Nothing stuck out at me as suspicious. After about forty minutes, I slipped out the back and left.

By the time I got to the funeral home our family had used for fifty years, dusk was falling and the Monterey Peninsula's sky was glowing pink and orange. I pulled into the parking lost just as the owner, Federico Montero, was locking the door of the building. He paused when he saw me and then took off his hat.

"I'm sorry, Miss Santella, for your loss."

"Thanks Mr. Montero. I know you're leaving, but is there any chance I can see him?"

He unlocked the door without a word and gestured for me to enter. He locked the door behind us and led me through the darkened rooms to a stairway to the basement. "I just finished up. I'm moving him upstairs in the morning for the viewing tomorrow night."

He didn't question why I wanted to see my brother before the viewing, just flicked on the harsh fluorescent lights and turned to go back up the stairs so I could be alone.

There was only one body downstairs, on a gurney in the corner. The funeral director's assortment of tools, including a variety of make-up bottles, was neatly put away on a shelf. Christopher looked like a big doll. As I came closer, it was hard to believe that empty shell had ever contained life. Anything that had made this flesh animated had long gone.

My brother looked like a pretty boy mannequin — hair dyed back to his natural glossy black, no stubble on the chiseled jaw and chin. Long, lush black eyelashes resting on high cheekbones. He was dressed in a black suit. Armani. The only jewelry was my mother's rosary clasped between his waxen hands. I hadn't known he had the rosary. I'd always wondered what had happened to it. It was something we often saw in my mother's delicate hands when she was worried about something — if my father was away on business or driving home in a thunder storm or when my grandmother was hospitalized from a stroke.

"You are going to be buried in Monterey."

Backing off a little, I waited, as if he were going to sit up and answer me.

I stared at him for a good ten minutes. I had nothing else to say. Instead, I searched my memory for snippets of the Christopher my mother had loved. I pushed back the lecherous looks he gave me in Santa Cruz the last time I saw him and tried to focus on the little boy who was so proud when my mother praised him for saying his alphabet or singing in the school play, or later, bringing home straight A's from boarding school.

The only time I'd ever seen a tender side of Christopher was when he was with my mother. I remembered one day being absolutely sick with jealousy watching Christopher play a complicated Bach piece on the piano with my mother beaming at him, so entranced she didn't even notice me in the room.

The look in her eyes as she watched Christopher was one I'd never seen before. She'd never looked at me that way. I had rushed into the room excited to show her a picture I had painted. But when I saw her face, my picture of a flower in a pot—which had seemed amazingly beautiful while I was making it—now looked like the babyish scribblings of a toddler. I held it behind my back and tried not to cry.

"Giada!" My mother's eyes took me in and she gave a long sigh. "Go change, dear. You have paint all over your best dress." I left the room, wadding the painting up in my tiny fists and then ripping it into smaller and smaller pieces.

I could never compete with Christopher. And now that he was out of the picture it didn't matter because my mother was long gone.

It was only when I heard footsteps upstairs that I was aroused from my daydreams. Then, I heard my name shouted.

Vito.

The funeral director had called my godfather. I glanced around. The funeral home was situated on a hill. A garage door was located at the other end of the room so the morgue could easily drop off the bodies. The garage door squealed open, showing part of a driveway and then a large expanse of woods. Footsteps pounded down the stairs. I was hiding in the alcove underneath them. The steps stopped. "She's gone."

"*Cazzo*!" My godfather shouted from the top of the stairs. "Split up. Find her."

After several people had gone running by, I heard the sound of the garage door closing and Federico mumbling something. Then I heard the jangle of keys as he went back up the stairs. I waited longer. Maybe a half hour after the building had grown quiet, I crept out from my hiding spot. My legs were cramped, but at least I hadn't been forced to hop into one of the empty coffins lining the wall, which had been one of my first thoughts.

I listened for about ten minutes and hearing nothing, crept up the stairs. I poked my head around the corner at the top. The place was empty. Peeking out the windows, I saw all the cars were gone, even my rental car. Shit. My godfather's goons had probably hotwired it and taken it with them to make sure I couldn't use it if I came out of the woods. Guess that I.D. was shot for now. And that rental car agency. The gig was up. My godfather knew I wasn't in Costa Rica. I'd have to be more careful than ever.

There was a garage full of cars at my parents' house, but that would be too hot. I knew Vito would have his men staked out there for sure.

The warrior's philosophy dictates that where he makes a conscious decision to not be a victim, he will prevail. Where he believes in his strength to overcome and persevere against seemingly impossible odds. The warrior does not give up or give in.

It took me about an hour to make it to Dante's mother's house by first heading toward the beach and then following the bike trail around to Pacific Grove. I hated to bring her into it, but I didn't know where else to turn to.

Standing in front of the large Tudor house I'd known as well as my own, I tried to finger comb my hair and brush off my clothes before I knocked on the door.

"Mrs. Marino?"

"Gia? *Mama mia*, child! What are you doing out here in the middle of the night?"

"I need your help."

She opened the door wider. “Come in.”

CHAPTER SEVENTEEN

THE NEXT MORNING POUNDING on my door woke me. I rolled over blinking to bring the clock into focus. It was already noon. I hadn't got back to the city and to my own bed until three in the morning.

Mrs. Marino hadn't asked me a single question. Only handed me the keys to her car when I told her I had no way to get back home to San Francisco.

My first stop last night when I got back to the city had been Darling's salon. I gave her the keys to Mrs. Marino's car and five hundred bucks. She assured me the car would be back in Mrs. Marino's driveway by dawn.

When I got back to my place, I'd stayed up late mulling over the business documents I'd seen at my godfather's place. I remembered the late notice I'd seen and made a note to try to get a hold of some more of the company's financial documents next.

The pounding on my door that had awoken me continued. I unearthed myself from Django's heavy bulk on my legs. He'd been so happy to see me—like I'd owned him forever — that I let him violate the "no bed" rule. Plus, I'd never really told him he couldn't get on the bed anyway, had I?

I pulled my green silk robe with the big dragon on the back around my shoulders and peered through the peephole. It was the little Vietnamese lady again.

Not bearing food this time. I cracked the door. She said something in Vietnamese and tried to see past me into the apartment.

"Ruff. Ruff?"

Oh. Django. I sighed and opened the door, gesturing for her to come in. She scampered in and raced over to the bed where Django was still sleeping. Some watch dog. She pressed her face to his and began scratching his ears and kissing his nose. She smiled at me and put her hand to her heart and then onto the dog. Yeah, I get it. You're an animal lover. Cool.

She looked around my apartment, taking in the bowls I used for dog food and water and then squinted at me and said something in Vietnamese. Of course, I didn't understand so she stood up and then bent her legs in a crouch and scrunched her face up as if she were straining. Oh.

"He uses the roof."

She shook her head no and left the apartment without a backward glance.

I took Django up to the roof, carrying a plastic bag to pick up his business. He sniffed around at the bare concrete and the air conditioning and heating units. I yawned and stretched in the streams of sunshine filtering through the light fog cover.

After I came back down the lady was pounding on my door again. When I cracked my door this time she came barreling in with a collar and leash and immediately snapped it on Django who began wiggling with excitement. She said something in Vietnamese.

"Fine. Yes, you can take him for a walk."

The woman beamed and leaned down to kiss Django on his long nose again.

"Hey, I'm Gia." I gestured to my chest. I figured it was high time for introductions.

"Thanh-Thanh," she said.

"Okay. Nice to meet you, Thanh-Thanh. This is Django." I pointed at the dog.

"Django," she tried to say it like I did, but I'm afraid it came out more like "Dang-O." That's okay. It didn't matter what she called him. The damn dog loved her. He was slobbering all over her and wiggling around like he'd never been for a walk before. Actually, who knows how long it had been since someone treated him like a real dog.

Thanh-Thanh and Django left for a walk and I'm not sure who was the more excited of the two.

I'd showered, done some Budo and had a smoothie for breakfast by the time my neighbor and dog returned.

"Doo, doo." Thanh-Thanh said.

"Fantastic," I said, trying not to sound sarcastic.

It was good to know someone else in my building liked the dog because lying in bed last night without any answers, it had become clear I'd need to make a trip to the charred remains of my parents' Geneva house.

I had some work to do before then, though, so I headed to the county offices to do a little research on the parcels of land my godfather had bought and the lone holdout.

At the county offices, I spent close to two hours scanning old property records. From what I could tell, this Stark woman had my godfather by the nutsack. He couldn't make a move without her property.

As I flipped through the records, I saw that the land had originally been called Carville because squatters had made homes out of old streetcars that had been abandoned in the dunes. The image of homeless people creating homes in abandoned streetcars triggered the memory I had been waiting for.

A shiver ran across my scalp as I remembered. This was why the other day I had alarms going off in my head about this deal. This development used to be called The Carville Condos. I remember it now. It was a proposal my godfather had made to my father maybe eight years ago and one that my father had shot down, publicly humiliating my godfather and causing them to be estranged for an entire year. At the time, I really couldn't see the appeal and why it was such a big deal.

My father's main argument was that he wouldn't go in and displace longtime homeowners who were against selling their home. I guess both my godfather and father had talked to more than twenty residents, but two people had refused to sell. The other property owner must have given in because now the lone hold-out was Jessica Stark.

Now that my father was out of the way, it seems within months of his death, my godfather had jumped on reviving this project, and somehow, probably using methods my father would have scorned, got the other reluctant homeowner to sell. The methods my godfather used were probably brute force. While my father had been friends with all the other Italian mobsters in Monterey, he'd always tried to walk the straight line. My godfather, God only knew. He was maybe more connected than I realized.

The other main obstacle my father had brought up when he opposed the plan was that the area was not zoned for multi-resident housing. I did a little more digging and found that had just changed. The city had recently approved the zoning change. I wondered what that had cost Vito in under the table money.

I left the county offices in a hurry. At home, I logged onto my father's company website. I still had access from when I worked there as a teen one summer. I searched all records dealing with the proposed San Francisco plant.

After another hour, I felt pretty sure my godfather had enough motivation to have killed my parents.

But one woman stood in his way.

Time to visit Jessica Stark.

THE TINY HOME WAS SHROUDED in fog when I arrived. Two window boxes full of begonias flanked the cheery red painted door. Mounds of sand and dirt surrounded the little gem of a house. Several backhoes and tractors parked in the adjacent dirt lot loomed as black silhouettes in the orange streetlights.

Mrs. Stark opened the door to my knock with a pistol pointing at my face. "Whoa," I said, putting my hands up and backing away. "I'm not sure you need the gun. I just want to talk to you."

"Nobody comes here just to talk. If you are here about me selling my house, you might as well leave now."

"I *am* here about you selling your house, but not because I want you to do that."

The woman behind the gun had a short gray bob, a paisley scarf flung around her neck and dangly earrings. She squinted her eyes at me and must have decided I was telling the truth because she kicked the door open.

"All right. You have ten minutes. I have to leave for my book club after that. We're reading Jess Walters' Beautiful Ruins and I need to save my breath for all the things I have to say about it."

I didn't know if that meant she liked it or hated it and right then, I didn't care.

Inside, Ms. Stark gestured to a green velvet couch in the living room. Bookshelves filled to overflowing and strung with white Christmas lights flanked three walls. In front of them were giant tropical plants also strung with small lights. A giant hookah sat on a leather stool near the couch.

The lady of the house was busying herself at a vintage chrome bar on wheels that sparkled with booze.

"Bourbon, okay?"

I'd gone cold turkey, but figured it would be inhospitable to refuse so I nodded. My mouth was watering before she even handed me the amber liquid.

Before she sat down, Mrs. Stark offered me a ceramic bowl with leather looking strips. "Beef jerky?"

"Sure," I said. Why the hell not?

She sat down and didn't wait for me to bring up the topic.

"I'm not selling. They can come in here and shoot me or run me over or whatever their mob tactics are, I'm staying here. That man is a bully."

I figured it was time to disclose who I was.

"That bully is my godfather. My name is Gia Santella."

She slammed her glass down on a rickety table near her chair. "Well, hells bells. And you say you don't want me to sell?"

"No, ma'am," I said. "Let me see what I can do. I only have a minority share in the business, but I'll try to work something out. I don't believe in running people out of their homes so some big corporation can make a few extra bucks. And my father, who started the company, didn't either."

"Well, that's a switch," Mrs. Stark said.

I stood and followed her into the kitchen with my glass and the empty ceramic bowl. One counter of the kitchen was overtaken by prescription bottles. I recognized one name. Eposin. I'd picked it up from the pharmacy once for a friend of mine before she died from cancer.

I held it up and raised an eyebrow.

"It's in my bones. I don't have long," she waved a hand at a calendar hanging on one wall. "Which reminds me I need to mark off yesterday. I'm already living past my due date—the six months the doctor predicted for me. I'm actually on day twenty past my 'deathday.'"

I exhaled and shook my head.

"That's why I'm not budging," Mrs. Stark said, walking me to the door. "I've lived here for thirty years. My husband and I bought this house right after we got married. We never had kids. I have no family left. He's gone and this house is all I have left. I intend to die here, Miss Santella."

I had nothing to say to that.

CHAPTER EIGHTEEN

LATER THAT NIGHT, I sat on the stoop and shared a bottle of gin with Ethel, the homeless lady with the paisley scarf. We passed the bottle back and forth, since my resolve to detox had derailed at Jessica Stark's house. I needed something to stop my mind from going where I didn't want it to go. Christopher's plastic-looking body. Images of my parents' bodies with bullets in their foreheads. Jessica Stark marking off the days that pass after her "deathday."

We sat there under the streetlight taking long pulls.

"What's your story, Ethel?"

She was quiet.

"It's okay," I said. "You don't have to talk about it. But if you want to, I'd like to know."

"I wasn't always like this," she said, looking away, down the street. "I used to have a place to live and all that. I grew up in Berkeley. Was going to go to school and everything, I just got hooked up with the wrong guy. I was only nineteen. He was handsome and charming, worked in San Francisco as a bus driver. On our first date, he brought me a dozen red roses. He told me he'd take care of me. I was so dumb. We got married at city hall one day when we were drunk. I moved in with him into a crappy little apartment I'd thought was heaven. At first. His version of taking care of me was to get drunk and beat me black and blue every night. He told me if I left him, he'd kill me. So, one night I waited until he was asleep and I killed him. I stabbed him with a steak knife. He didn't die right away. Then I called the police. I spent fifteen years at Susanville. When I got out, I had nowhere to go. I stayed at a little hotel for a while. Then the money ran out."

I pressed my lips together and nodded.

A young thug walking funny to keep his pants from falling off eyed us from the other side of the street. "Hey!" I shouted.

He kept walking.

"Hey!" I tried again. "Hey you! Come here!"

He paused looking around until he realized we were talking to him.

"Yeah, you."

He crossed the street, looking around as if he expected a trap.

"Got any ganga, my friend." My words were slurred.

"Why you want to know?"

I took out a hundred-dollar bill. "Come on, man. Give us a spliff. I'll trade you."

He looked around again, warily.

"How I know you not the cops?"

"Look at us," I said, gesturing to me and Ethel, who cackled loudly at his words. "We look like the law?"

"Guess not." He rummaged around and came up with a joint, reaching for my hundred-dollar bill.

"Is it laced?" I said, pulling the money just out of his reach.

"No. It ain't dusted."

"You sure?" I asked, giving him the stink eye.

"Yeah, man." I handed him the bill. He started to walk away. "Wait. Got a light?"

He rolled his eyes and lit the joint before he turned and left, muttering something about crazy white women.

Ethel and I stayed talking and finishing our second bottle of gin until the sky started to lighten with pink streaks.

"Hey, Ethel."

"Hmmm?" she answered sleepily. It had grown cold as the dawn broke. The fog rolling in turned the air damp and heavy. I pulled my scarf tighter.

"What do you think about running a little errand for me this morning?"

"Mmm hmmm."

"I need you to deliver a message for me. It's in Chinatown. I'll make it worth your while."

"Mmmm kay," she said.

"Be back in a sec."

I raced upstairs and wrote a note to Kato. I asked him to meet me in the back office of Darling's salon around midnight. I told him I'd leave the back door unlocked. I wanted to run my plan by him. Downstairs, I handed Ethel the envelope with Kato's address written on the outside.

"I'm hitting the sack," I started for the door, but felt a stab of guilt watching Ethel pull her rags tighter around her body. "Hey, Ethel, you want to crash at my place for a few hours?"

"No. I'm fine," she mumbled.

"You sure?"

"Yep."

"Hey, you don't usually sleep out here do you?"

"Nope."

I wondered where she normally spent her nights and felt even more guilty when I realized I'd kept her up all night drinking.

I WOKE UP THAT AFTERNOON close to four and quickly pulled on some wadded-up jeans so I could run down the stairs and see if Ethel had delivered my message. I flung open the door and saw her sitting there on a stack of cardboard boxes half asleep.

"Ethel?"

She gave a loud snore. I'd let her sleep. I walked to the bar for a grilled cheese sandwich and soda and read the paper for an hour. Not much new.

Today was Christopher's funeral. The only person I knew who might attend was the person I suspected wanted me dead — my godfather.

It was scary to feel this alone in the world. Briefly, I thought about calling Dante. I'd written a long, rambling letter to him and left it in his mother's car. I didn't give any details but told him someone wanted me dead and for him to stay out of it and trust nobody. I hoped he listened to my advice.

Once this was all over, I was going to take a long weekend and stay with him in Calistoga. I needed to be around someone who loved me. Now that my godfather was dead to me, I only had two people in my life who were as close as family. Kato and Dante. I could see Kato, but would have to wait until I could see Dante again. Sometimes blood wasn't thicker than water.

WHEN I RETURNED TO my place, Ethel was sitting up on the sidewalk. I was anxious to meet with Kato.

"How'd it go?"

"Here," she said trying to hand the eighty bucks back to me and the envelope. "He wasn't there."

"No, keep it," I said distractedly, pushing the money back at her. "What do you mean he wasn't there?" Kato had never missed a work day at the dojo for the past two years.

"Big closed sign on the door. Note said something about 'family emergency.' "

My heart slowed and a chill ran over my scalp. I reached down and grabbed Ethel's wrist. "Are you certain? Are you sure it said 'family emergency?'"

She looked at me wide eyed and nodded.

I turned and ran toward Market Street. I hadn't even brushed my teeth yet.

The warrior knows that looking beyond oneself to care for others is the ultimate goal of living Budo for life. That self-improvement is important, but improving one's self is crucial to help others on their own journeys.

On Market, it took me ten minutes to hail a cab. Several passed me by. I knew with my ratty hair and clothes I didn't look like a very good fare. It wasn't until I stepped right in front of a cab that it screeched to a halt. I threw open the door and spit out Kato's address in the Mission, flashing three twenties. "Go as fast as you can."

When we pulled onto Kato's street, I saw a long black car parked in front of his house. I told the cab driver to back up and go around the block to the street behind Kato's. The street was nearly interchangeable with Kato's: old houses, some with chipped paint and old cars parked in the yards, but also with kid's bicycles propped up against porches, and small, neatly tended flower beds. "Stop here." I opened the door, handed him a twenty and told him he'd get the other two twenties when I returned as long as he waited. I walked until I was at the house that butted up against Kato's backyard. An older woman in rollers and a flowered housecoat sat out on the front porch petting a cat and sipping a soda pop.

"You know Kato?"

She didn't answer just nodded slowly.

"Why's the black car out front?"

"Didn't I see you at that Fourth of July barbecue Kato had last summer?"

"Yes!" I said a little too excitedly. "Yes, we're friends. What's going on?"

"Dunno. Susie dropped the boys off here two hours ago. Told my daughter to take them to her folk's house in Berkeley. Susie was going to the hospital. Something happened to Kato."

I didn't even say thank you, just raced back to the waiting cabbie. "San Francisco General."

CHAPTER NINETEEN

I WAS OUT OF BREATH by the time I got to the family waiting room at the hospital. It was filled with people staring off into space or sitting in huddled groups hugging and crying. Kato's wife sat alone with her head in her hands.

"Susie?"

When she looked up, I barely recognized her grief-ravaged face. Her skin was even paler than normal and her eyes were red from crying. She stood and hugged me. "Gia. He might not make it." Her body shook with sobs.

I held her for a few seconds and then led her back to her seat by the hand.

"What happened?" I said, my stomach doing somersaults.

"I'm not sure," she said. "I got a call from one of his students."

When Kato's first student showed up fifteen minutes early, he'd found Kato's crumpled body on the floor of the dojo, she said. He had been severely beaten. A heavy steel pipe with blood on it was found nearby. The student's early arrival, before the dojo opened to the public, had probably interrupted the attack and saved Kato's life. Police had found witnesses who said a group of four men had been seen fleeing out the back door of the dojo within seconds of the student making the 911 call.

Kato was in surgery. It looked like he had taken a severe blow to the head and also suffered broken ribs and a punctured lung.

Why would someone hurt Kato? It didn't make any sense. I caught my breath. Unless, it had something to do with me. I drew back from hugging Susie and took a closer look at the other people in the waiting room.

Nobody I knew. None of my godfather's thugs, just worried family members.

"Susie?"

She blew her nose and looked at me.

"Did you know there is a big black car in front of your house?"

Her eyes grew wide and she shook her head.

"I don't know for sure, but I think the people who are after me might have done this to Kato." I closed my eyes. I felt sick to my stomach even saying that.

Susie wrapped her arms around me. "It's not your fault."

"I think it might be," I said opening my eyes. I took her by the shoulders. "You can't go home. You have to go to your parents. I think you're safe here in the hospital, but don't come home. Go to your parents and stay there until I call you."

She sniffled. "Okay, Gia. I don't think anyone would hurt me, but if you say so."

"I do," I said. "I just know this is connected to someone trying to find me. And these people—I used to think women and children were off limits—but I just don't know anymore. I'd rather you were safe. I have to go now, but please promise me, you'll be careful."

She looked at me solemnly and nodded.

Just then the elevator door dinged. I ducked back into the doorway, grabbed my compact mirror out of my bag and stuck it into the hall at waist level. By holding it just right I could see the nurse's desk. Two men in dark suits were talking to the nurse on duty. "Call 911 if those two men in suits even try to talk to you," I told Susie and slipped out a side door of the waiting room toward the stairwell.

I took the back stairs out of the hospital, wishing I had grabbed my gun before I ran out of the house this morning. Being alone on the stairs creeped me out. I'd just read last month that a patient who had disappeared was found dead in the stairwell. She'd been there for three weeks before someone found her body. But my anger overpowered my fear.

I walked eight blocks away from the hospital before I boarded a bus back to the Tenderloin.

ETHEL WASN'T AT HER usual spot outside.

Upstairs, Django greeted me with enthusiasm and I buried my face in his fur for a few seconds taking deep, gulping breaths. I hadn't been to church since I was a kid, but I suddenly wanted to go light a candle for Kato. The thought of his dying sent such a tremor of fear through me, I could barely breathe.

I'd go to a Catholic church I'd seen around the corner and light a candle and say a prayer for him.

I took Django for a walk. He about lost his mind when I picked up the leash Thanh-Thanh had bought for him. Despite feeling sick to my stomach with worry over Kato, I couldn't help but smile at the damn dog's enthusiasm.

I made my plans for the night. I'd walk Django, light a candle at a church, and then sneak back into the hospital to check on Kato's condition.

Having a plan seemed the only thing that would keep me from falling into my bed and not getting up for the next month. I felt such a heavy wave of despair hit me. It was all too much.

CHAPTER TWENTY

I'D PASSED SAINT BONIFACE a few times in my wanderings around the Tenderloin. It looked like it belonged on a beach in Mexico with its soaring yellow towers and pink accents and dozens of looming stained glass windows. It was an object of wonder and beauty in one of the worst San Francisco neighborhoods.

I gingerly pulled on the door. I hadn't been to church since my parents' funeral. A tiny part of me worried I'd burst into flames when I walked in, but instead I was stopped dead, frozen by one of the most stunning altars I'd ever seen. The entire church was full of swooping arches, inlaid gilt and gold and beautiful pictures of saints and the virgin Mary and Jesus. From the floor up everything was either gold or a myriad of brilliant gem tones. The floor was plush red carpet. So many murals and gold and stained-glass windows.

It wasn't until I had taken a few steps inside that I realized something was off.

A soft rumbling filled the church. It took me a moment to realize what it was.

Dozens of people snoring.

That's when the smell hit me. Along with the usual incense of the Catholic church, which I remembered from my youth there was also a faint unpleasant stench of unwashed bodies and perspiration.

The drone of snoring was accompanied by shuffling and coughs and the occasional snort. But I could see no one.

Slight movement in one of the pews caught my eye. As I grew closer, I saw.

Each pew held a body curled up for the night.

Most were wrapped in dingy gray or brown blankets, but there was also an occasional flowered or checked blanket. I did the math in my head, counting the rows of pews. There must have been more than one hundred homeless people sleeping in this church.

I didn't know whether to laugh or cry.

It was so unexpected and so *right.*

Above all the sleeping bodies, thirty feet in the air, a bevy of painted saints in brilliant colors looked down from the ceiling upon these people seeking shelter in a house of God.

I heard a throat clear at my shoulder and wasn't surprised when I turned and saw that instead of a priest, a man in monk's robes was at my side.

"Welcome, sister. Are you here for confession?"

"Uh, no," I said, feeling guilty since I hadn't stepped foot in a church since my parent's funeral. "I'm here to pray and light a candle for a very ill friend. He might not make it. He was beat up and I think it was my fault." I choked the words out. There. That was a close to a confession as I was getting on this night.

"Please, his name. I will add him to my prayers."

"Thank you, brother. His name is Kato." He didn't blink when I said the name, only led me to an alcove with a statue of the Virgin Mary. When I crouched down on the kneeler, my jacket opened and my gun gleamed in the candlelight. The monk's eyes rested on the shiny metal for a moment before he raised his eyes to me.

"Good luck with whatever you are seeking, sister. Stay safe."

I thanked him and he turned and left. I stuffed twenty bucks into the box used to collect money for candle lighting. I lit a candle and said a prayer. I was rusty. I hadn't prayed for a long time, but I still believed that if there was a God, he could not turn his back on somebody as good and righteous as Kato.

After my prayer, I stood and as if in a daze once again took in all the homeless people seeking shelter in this ethereally beautiful church. I stuffed a hundred-dollar bill in the offering box and then got out another and wadded that up until it fit in the narrow opening. It wasn't much, but I'd be back.

As I left, I saw a head wrapped in a familiar paisley scarf. Ethel.

I GOT OFF THE BUS A few blocks away from San Francisco General and walked to the emergency entrance. It was late. The middle of the night. I knew any visiting hours had ended hours ago. I walked in the back door like I knew where I was going and what I was doing and headed for the back stairwell again.

On the sixth floor, I cracked the door and looked into the hallway in front of me. Empty. I slowly closed the door behind me. The area was hushed and quiet. I peeked in as I snuck past the family waiting area. At the nurse's station, one woman with short gray hair was talking quietly on the phone. She held up one finger asking me to wait. I smiled gratefully. I'd expected her to immediately kick me out. I shrunk back and leaned against a wall, trying to look like I wasn't paying attention to much. Finally, she hung up.

"Visiting hours are over," she said and raised an eyebrow.

"Yeah, I'm sorry, I know. I just was wondering if you could check a patient's condition for me?" A note of begging had crept into my voice and I didn't care. *Please, help me.*

"Are you a family member?"

I knew I could lie, but I decided just to tell her the truth.

"No. I have no family. He's as close as I have." I didn't mean to play on her sympathy but my voice did choke on a sob as I said it.

She gave me a long look. "Patient name?"

"Kato Mazuka."

She tapped on her keyboard. "He's in stable condition in the ICU. Just moved there from recovery."

"Um, I'm sorry to not know this, but when you say stable, does that mean, like fair condition or critical or what?"

She looked over her glasses at me. "It lists him as critical, but I think he's regained consciousness. Although I'm not really supposed to tell you that."

"Thanks." I gave a sigh of relief. He was awake.

"Also, he's in room 412. But I didn't tell you that, either." She winked and I smiled gratefully and headed for the stairs.

CHAPTER TWENTY-ONE

I PUNCHED THE WALL periodically as I raced down the hospital stairs until my knuckles were bleeding.

I was right. My godfather's goons had beaten Kato nearly to death because he refused to tell them where I was. He had only been conscious for a few minutes when I first entered, waiting for the nurse to look down at her chart before I snuck into his room. It hurt just to look at his bandaged and swollen face and all the tubes hooking him to an assortment of machines.

He basically saw me, mumbled, "I didn't tell them where you were, *Gia-san*," and fell back unconscious or asleep. I didn't know which.

The fury inside me sent me flying out his door, ready to scream or explode, I wasn't sure which. How dare someone beat up my best friend in an effort to find me. My godfather must have lost his mind.

I spent the night pacing the rooftop of my building, wrapped in a blanket from my bed, searching the misty skies of San Francisco trying to figure out where I should turn next. It looked like a visit to Geneva was in order. I wanted to talk to the widow of the forensic pathologist who falsified my parents' autopsy results, the woman who had written me the letter. Maybe she would have some clue who paid off her husband. I wanted a little more proof before I confronted my godfather. I couldn't live with killing him unless I knew for sure he was behind all the death and tragedy in my life. A part of me still loved him desperately. The soft part of the me. The part that wanted to curl up and die instead of fight. I pushed that part of me deep down inside.

The warrior may be shattered in mind, body, and spirit and yet will not give up. The warrior knows that one's strength lies in many areas, spiritual as well as physical and the melding of the two creates true power.

The next morning, Ethel was back in her regular spot.

I slung my backpack onto my shoulder. I had a concealed money belt under my jeans that contained cash, my fake passport, driver's license, and photocopies of the Italian property deeds. I'd given Thanh-Thanh an extra key and mimed that I was getting on an airplane and would be gone for a few days. She figured out through my sign language, pointing to Django's leash and food bowl and holding up my fingers, that I needed her to walk and feed Django while I was gone. She thudded her chest and nodded so fiercely, I figured she got the point. At least I hoped so. My plane left in two hours. I crouched down by Ethel.

"Sorry, Gia. I tried to deliver your message," she said.

"I know. You did good. It's not your fault," I said. Her eyes were bloodshot and her speech a bit slurred even though it was only ten in the morning. She must have used some of my money for that bottle of vodka I saw peeking out of her backpack. I leaned closer. "Ethel, look at me, this is important." Her eyes rolled over to mine. "When you went to the dojo. Did anyone see you come back here? Did anyone follow you?"

"No, no, Gia. I did just what you told me. I took two buses, that one to North Beach and then another one to get back here. I made sure nobody got off at my stop and no cars were following the bus. I watched. I done just like you told me."

"Good job," I said, standing. "I'm going to be gone for a few days. You want to stay in my place?"

"I got a place to stay. I'm good."

"You sure? My place will just be sitting there empty."

"No, no I'm fine." I wondered if she was going to tell me she slept at Saint Boniface or whether she liked keeping that secret. I didn't want to intrude on her privacy so I didn't mention seeing her there the night before. For a fleeting moment, I wondered what would happen if I paid for her to go to rehab. Was there any hope? Could I help her? I remembered something Dante told me once "You can't save someone from themselves."

But I wondered if I needed to try.

"Ethel?" I paused and waited.

"Yes?" She looked up and gave me a sweet smile.

"You ever think about kicking?"

Her eyebrows creased together.

"You know," I said. "Maybe go somewhere where they can help you stop drinking and stuff?" I looked away. I waited a few seconds and looked back at her. She was staring right at me.

"Nah. Gia. I want to drink. I want to do what I want to do and what I want to do is drink."

"I like booze too, Ethel." I said. "Maybe if you stopped drinking, maybe you could be my roommate and we could find you a job at my friend's salon or something. She's awfully nice. We could ..."

I was trying to figure out a way to tell her that her life could be better. But how could I say that without insulting everything she was right now?

"Gia," she waited for me to look her in the eye. "I may be homeless, but I'm free."

I thought about that for a second. There was nothing I could say. I pressed my lips together tightly and nodded.

"Okay. You let me know if you change your mind. I know some people."

She looked away but I saw her acknowledge what I said with a slight nod.

I gave her one last look before I walked toward Market Street so I could hail a cab to the airport.

CHAPTER TWENTY-TWO

MY PLANE TOUCHED DOWN in Geneva at dawn. I'd slept through most of the flight after helping myself to several mini bottles of red wine. I woke to the flight attendant's announcing our imminent arrival and lunged for my giant bottle of water. My tongue was sticking to the roof of my mouth and my pulse was pounding a Congo line behind my eyes. Drinking on an overseas flight was one of the worst ideas I'd had in a long time.

With only my backpack, I ripped through customs, arranged for a rental car and headed toward my hotel in the center of town. I loved downtown Geneva with its stately old buildings, café tables on the sidewalks, and wrought iron balconies overlooking the street.

Checking in was an exercise in practicing my rusty French. I probably came across like a preschooler, but I got what I needed from the desk clerk.

The small room had a tiny, white desk with an upholstered chair, a white-framed bed with flowered bedspread, a dresser, a coffeemaker, and a bowl of fruit. No TV, which was fine by me.

I showered, ate an apple, some grapes, and drank about a pot of coffee before I headed out. I dressed as demurely as I could, in simple black pants, a white blouse and black blazer. I pulled my hair back in a low ponytail, grabbed some dark sunglasses and kept the makeup to a minimum. My rental car was ostentatious enough.

I missed driving my Ferrari, so I'd rented a Tesla Signature Roadster. I realized this was drawing attention to myself, but by the time word got back to my godfather — and that's assuming he did have spies here in Geneva — I'd be long gone.

My plan was to show up at the widow's house at eight–supper time–and surprise her. I hoped she'd open her doors wide. She'd put her address on the envelope for a reason, right?

Until then, I would take the Tesla for a spin. I'd been mellow on the drive from the rental agency to the hotel—I'd been more interested in the spectacular views of Lake Geneva including the famous *Jet d'eau* — a fountain in the middle of the lake that spouted water more than four hundred feet in to the air.

But now I itched to see what was under the hood. I was going to take the Tesla for a test drive through the nearby French Alps.

I grew up going to the races at Laguna Seca raceway. When I turned sixteen my parents bought me an orange twin turbo Dodge Viper and enrolled me in the Skip Barber Racing Course at the racetrack.

As soon as I learned to race, I decided I also wanted to learn how to work on cars. I got a job that summer in the pit crew at Laguna Seca, helping the mechanics change tires and refuel the cars. I think for a while my parents suspected I was the kind of girl who didn't like boys, but that ended the night they found the thirty-year-old French racecar driver in my bed. They were supposed to be flying out to Europe that day but the flight was grounded due to fog. Thank God my mom was there to stop my father from killing the poor guy on the spot. He escaped with his clothes in his hands. I never heard from him again.

After that, my mother gave me the birth control talk privately while my dad publicly announced that he would harm any man or boy that touched his teenage daughter. My father must have suspected Dante was gay before I ever had a clue because that was one guy my father always let me spend time around.

Today, I didn't attract as much attention as I thought driving the Tesla through town. There was some international finance meeting and it looked like billionaires from across the world had convened in Geneva solely to putt around in their luxury sports cars. I spotted five Ferraris, including one Ferrari 458 Italia Spider, three Lamborghini Gallardo LP 560-4 Bicolores, and even a McLaren MP4-12C. The dozens of Porsches, Jaguars and Mercedes seemed provincial next to the higher-end luxury race cars.

Needless to say, nobody batted an eye at my Tesla.

As soon as I left the city limits, my spirits lifted. Driving fast had always been my therapy. Before long I was hugging the mountain curves along the Alps that served as the natural boundary between three countries — Switzerland, France, and Italy. I steeled myself for my visit that night. I needed to get proof that my godfather was a killer and then I'd have to take care of it myself. I was the only one left to avenge my family's name.

The thought made my stomach hurt, but I knew I had to do it for my father. He would've expected no less of me. There was a reason he wanted me to study karate, learn to fix cars, and shoot guns when I was only fifteen. He knew that someday these skills would come in handy. He had prepared me well.

I brushed aside these thoughts and pressed my foot to the gas pedal. As my speedometer's numbers increased, my thoughts flew out the window into the wind and I concentrated on the rush that speed gave me.

I hopped onto the Route des Grandes Alpes, also known as the N902, which climbed higher and higher, past Bourg St. Maurice, until the air was so cold I had to crank the car's heater.

One of my books on Budo had talked about how for many American's driving the freeway had become an act of meditation. In Japan, the book said, people reached a meditative state through the tea ceremony. But when Americans tried to imitate this, they were unable to achieve that subconscious state. The theory was that for the Japanese, the tea ceremony was so ingrained in their culture and life that when they performed the ceremony, their minds and bodies naturally went into auto pilot – they did it entirely without thinking and as a result, their thoughts wandered and they were able to achieve that meditative state.

In America, the book said, the activity that had become so rote and automatic was driving. So much so that many people did it on auto pilot and achieved a state of meditation. At the time I read it, this theory made perfect sense. More than once, I had headed on a familiar freeway and completely missed my exit without realizing it because I had been daydreaming, or meditating, or whatever subconscious state you could call it.

That's one reason I embraced driving as my own unique therapy.

On this day, in a million-dollar car, on one of the most scenic roads in the world, I really didn't take much of it in. Instead, I turned inward, going over everything I knew about my parents' deaths hoping that some little tidbit that had escaped me would surface. I sifted back through a lifetime of memories about my godfather, trying to understand why he would turn on my family like this. Nothing made sense. I realized I could think about it for the rest of my life without understanding.

It wasn't until I reached the stretch of N902 called the Col de I'Iseran that I realized I should probably find a spot to turn around and head back. I didn't want to be late to the widow's house. Even though she wasn't expecting me.

CHAPTER TWENTY-THREE

THE FORENSIC PATHOLOGIST had lived in a modern home with sweeping views of Lake Geneva. Driving to the home, I tried not to look at a long, unmarked driveway as I passed it. I hadn't been there for years, but I knew the tree-lined driveway would lead to the charred remains of my parents' house. I'd deal with that later.

Every once in a while, I caught a glimpse of the backside of the doctor's house from the winding road leading up to it. The backside faced the lake. The setting sun reflected off the wall of windows overlooking the water. As I got closer I could tell that a forest of large trees surrounded the house on the other three sides. A Koi pond sat in the center of a large circular driveway.

It looks like the doctor had definitely kept up with the Joneses. I wondered if the opulence was mainly a result of him being on the mob payroll to falsify autopsy results.

A maid answered the door. After seeing the house, I don't know why this surprised me. The woman was about my age, a very beautiful blond woman dressed in a gray pencil skirt, black button-up blouse and frilly maid apron over that.

"I'm here to see Mrs. Gutmann. I'm not expected. Can you please tell her that Giada Santella is here to see her?" If anything, I hoped my last name would spark some interest.

Without any expression, the woman asked me to wait and silently glided down the hall in her ballet slippers. When the woman returned, she gave me a slightly annoyed look.

"Mrs. Gutmann has just sat down to dinner."

Yup. Why I'd arrived at eight on the dot. I tried to look pleasant.

"Fortunately," the woman continued, making it clear that it was actually *not* fortunate. "Mrs. Gutmann is dining alone tonight and has asked you to join her."

She turned on her heel and began walking down the hall to another doorway without waiting to see if I was following. I waited a few seconds just to see if she would look. When she didn't, I caught up, my heels clicking loudly behind her silent glide.

An open door revealed a brightly lit room with a glass topped table and sideboards filled with flowers. At one end of the table, a woman with an elegant silver chignon nodded at me without getting up. Her blue eyes took me in from head to toe as she gestured at the spot to her right.

"Pleased to meet you, Mrs. Gutmann," I said nodding my head at her. "I apologize for the unannounced visit."

Mrs. Gutmann acknowledged my apology with the slightest downward dip of her chin. "I see my letter ended up in your hands. As planned." Her voice was soft and I detected a note of sadness. "I'm sorry for your loss."

I dipped my own chin in acknowledgment.

"You said 'as planned,' but how did you know I would be the one to find it?"

"Miss Santella, I only had my man slip the letter into the door after he saw you enter the house."

I'd assumed the letter had been on the floor when I came into the house. I never considered that someone had slipped it through the mail slot *after* I'd arrived.

"You wanted me to get it?"

"I am an orphan, as well, Miss Santella," she said, waving at a woman carrying two soup bowls in. After the soup was placed in front of us — a fragrant shimmer of broth — she continued. "I wanted you to be the one to find out about the deception."

"Why? Why did your husband do that?" I cringed after I asked it. I wondered if she would kick me out before the main course.

"Apparently, his business was failing and he was too ashamed to ask me for help," the woman said. "I inherited, like you, more money than I will possibly ever need, but my husband's pride prevented him from telling me we needed the money. So, he decided to borrow some — from the wrong people. And as you may be aware of, once you are granted a favor by these people, they don't hesitate to ask you for favors in return."

She lifted one eyebrow.

I knew who those people were – Italian mafia. Their favors came at a very high cost. My dad had warned me about this once when I became friends with the daughter of a powerful Monterey attorney.

"We are polite to the Capazzos, but we are not friends," my father had told me. "One day you will understand why."

It wasn't until I was a teenager that my father explained how difficult it was for him to remain separate from the Monterey mafia scene because he was a *paesano* from the same area of Sicily. He told me that my godfather was the one who kept the peace and kept our family from being controlled by the mafia and yet still able to make a living in the seafood business. I didn't really understand what he meant at the time.

But now, at Mrs. Gutmann's table, I knew exactly what she was talking about. Her husband had been indebted to the mafia and when it had become too unreasonable, he had taken his own life.

"Does anyone else know about this?"

"No," the woman said, gingerly patting her rose-lipsticked mouth with a white linen napkin. "The reason I contacted you was that I always liked your mother."

My heart beat faster. "You knew my mother?" My voice squeaked a little.

"Only from various functions here and there in Geneva, but your mother was a lady of grace and class and always struck me as something better than ... this mafia business."

The doors swung open and two women came in carrying plates of seafood, fresh clams, and scallops in a white wine sauce along with tiny pieces of toasts to soak up the juices. Mrs. Gutmann dipped her fork into the dish and I followed suit.

After we ate, she gestured that I should grab my wine glass and join her on the deck overlooking the lake. The night air was warm. We sank into plush couches on the deck and watched the sun set to the west.

"I suppose you are here looking for some answers," Mrs. Gutmann said, lighting a slim cigarette from a gold case. She didn't offer me one.

"I need to know who killed my parents. And why," I said, staring out at the lights of Geneva across the lake. "I think I might know but I'm looking for proof before I act on it."

"And you think you might find that proof here?"

"I was hoping to." Now that I was halfway across the world, I started to doubt why I'd come here at all. What had I expected to find?

She stood up, smoking and standing at the rail overlooking the lake.

"I can tell you one thing and one thing only," she said still facing the lake. "But it might mean everything you ever believed was a lie. Do you want to unearth the past in that way?" She paused. "My dear, I've learned a lot in my sixty-five years here on this earth, but the most important lesson that I hold dear to my heart is that ignorance can be bliss. However, as much as my heart knows this, my brain will never settle for knowing less than the truth. I suspect you are like me. It makes me sad for you. The people who are happiest in this life are not like you and me. But I like you and I respect your need to know."

She turned to me so quickly I nearly jumped. "If you are certain, I can only point you in the right direction. That is all."

CHAPTER TWENTY-FOUR

MY HEART WAS RACING. I didn't know if it was from the bottle of wine we'd shared or from the knowledge that this woman was going to give me the answers I sought.

I closed my eyes for only a second and then opened them, nodding vigorously. "I need to know."

"You will find what you need in Sicily."

I waited. But she turned on her heel and left saying, "I've said too much. The maid will see you out."

"Wait," I tried to follow her, but she disappeared into a small doorway off the deck. The door was locked from the other side. I pounded on it. "Mrs. Gutmann. Please. Please tell me more. Was that all you were going to tell me? I need your help. I need more than that."

The maid appeared at the door. "It's time for you to go."

By this time, it was dark. But I didn't want to put off visiting the remains of my parent's house.

When I got to the end of the long driveway, my headlights shone on a hulking mass that had once been my parents' love nest. Only half the house had burned. I guess that is how they were able to find my parents' bodies. I'd been told they had burned to death in their beds and that the fire had taken place in the dead of night. But now, with the car's lights shining on the house, I realized that the portion of the house that was still standing included their bedroom.

I walked around to the back of the house and let myself in through an unlocked door. All the windows had been smashed. I could see clearly thanks to a nearly full moon that seemed to dangle right above the house.

Inside, the floors were littered with jagged glass. Squatters and thieves had looted the house long ago. Nothing was left except piles of empty food containers and other trash. Not a painting was left on the wall. Not a bit of furniture. I made my way up the stairs to my parents' bedroom, heart racing, wishing I had been able to bring my gun to Geneva.

I stood in the doorway to my parents' room. The glass walls that overlooked Lake Geneva had been shattered. Pieces of broken furniture lay on the ground two stories below. Trash and cigarette butts littered the floor. I walked in circles around where their bed had been, squinting and looking for some clue. The once beautiful mahogany floor was stained. But one stain looked darker than the other. Was it blood? If so, it was just to the side of where my parents' bed had been. My stomach flip flopped.

That's when I noticed the blood spatter. It was on the wall where their headboard would have been on their bed. Right at that spot, two large stains sprinkled the wall in starbursts. I leaned in and saw something; some substance stuck to the wall. I jerked away and threw up all over the wood floor, splattering white wine and clams and scallops and broth everywhere. I leaned over, my hands on my knees, until I was retching in dry heaves. Then, when I was finished, I wiped my mouth on my sleeve, stood up straight, and, with my legs shaking uncontrollably, headed for the door.

I'd seen enough.

CHAPTER TWENTY-FIVE

I CALLED DANTE FROM the airport in Rome. I'd reluctantly turned in my rental car and bought a train ticket to Sicily.

When Dante answered, I launched into conversation.

"I need information on a Mateo Antonio Turricci. I looked him up online the other day at my hotel, but didn't find jack," I said.

"Your hotel? Where are you? Are you going to tell me why you disappeared? My mother said you showed up at her house one night? But when I went to your apartment, the place was empty and looked like a tornado had struck. Gia, what the hell is going on?"

He was clearly angry. I didn't blame him, but I also didn't have time.

"Listen I love you. I'm sorry. My parents were murdered. Christopher was murdered. And someone wants me dead. I'm in Europe to get some answers. Please. My train leaves soon. I need your help."

He let out a big sigh and I knew he'd forgiven me.

"I'll get Matt on it. He can use his State Department contacts to dig up some dirt." There was a pause. "Are you going to tell me anything else?"

"I've probably told you too much. I'm even worried that Matt poking around might be dangerous. I just don't know what else to do."

"I thought your parents died in a fire."

"I'm sorry. I can't say anything else."

"Are you sure?" He sounded worried.

"I was just at their house last night. I saw pieces of their brain on the wall. Yes, I'm goddamn sure."

"Oh, Jesus, Gia. I'm so sorry."

"I'm sorry for snapping at you. I'm just really tired and ... I don't know." *Scared.*

"It's okay. I'm so sorry you had to see that." He paused. I could hear him inhale sharply. "Gia, maybe you should let someone else handle this. My mother said that you looked ... well, not like yourself."

"Tell her I'm fine. The less you know, the better. I promise I'll tell you everything as soon as I can."

A group of young men on scooters zoomed by, drowning out Dante's voice for a few seconds.

"— I don't like this at all," he said. "Gia, the autopsy report showed they died in a fire. I know you saw something there, but I'm worried that somebody is using you, maybe trying to get your money or something. You are very vulnerable right now. And maybe a bit more likely to be open to suggestion."

"You don't believe me? After I just told you I saw brains and blood on the wall?" It came out like a shriek. He thought I was imagining the whole thing?

"Gia, I want to believe you. I really do."

"It doesn't matter if you believe me or not, I still need your help." The line was silent. "Please, Dante? Just do this for me." I knew I was pleading and didn't care.

"I'll see what I can find out. Be careful."

"I'll call you when I get to Sicily." I hung up before he could answer.

I then dialed Susie to check that her family was safe. She said that Kato was going to be released this week. He was doing much better, she said.

A tiny particle of the guilt I was carrying around was released, but the weight on my back felt about the same. I wouldn't be able to rest until I knew for sure who was killing—or trying to kill—the people I loved.

ON THE TRAIN, I FOUND an empty compartment, locked the door, turned out the lights and decided I'd try to sleep. I hadn't slept worth a damn the night after visiting my parent's house. The train wasn't scheduled to arrive in the Southern Italian town of Milazzo until morning. From there, I'd take the ferry across to Sicily.

During the night, as I slept to the rocking movement of the train, I had an erotic dream about Bobby that turned into a horror movie. I thought I'd blocked him out of my mind forever. But my dream told me otherwise. In it, we were making love when I realized that Christopher's cold dead body was in bed with us. When I jumped out of bed in fright, Christopher sat up and laughed at me, a long, evil laugh. I woke, heart pounding to the sound of the train wheels clattering on the tracks.

Once the fright wore off, I thought about Bobby and his mouth and his hands. Longing coursed through me so strongly, I was tempted to go seek out a lover in the restaurant car — maybe some Italian businessman having a nightcap.

But I knew I should try to get more sleep. I had no idea what awaited me in Sicily and I wanted to be prepared. If that were even possible.

Sicily wasn't a big island, but it wasn't small, either. Without knowing what I was looking for, I might as well have been on my way to the Congo.

IN THE MORNING, I STUDIED my mother's land deeds while I munched on a cannoli and sipped an espresso in the restaurant car. Mateo Antonio Turricci had given my mother what looked like the deed to a house and several adjacent properties.

Before I stepped onto the ferry from Calabria to Sicily, I called Dante.

"Any luck?"

"Gia!" He sounded like he'd been waiting for my call. "That guy is bad news. The State Department guy told Matt that his file was classified. CIA eyes only. He's dangerous. I think you should leave your investigations up to the experts and come home. I think you're getting in over your head."

I laughed. Dante had always been overprotective of me. At least now he believed me.

"It's fine. I'm pretty sure the guy was my mother's guardian after her parents died. He left her a boatload of land. I'm actually hoping he's going to help me find out what happened to her. As soon as he hears what really happened, he'll be on my side. If he is powerful — maybe mafia — then that's even better. He'll make shit happen. Don't worry about me, sweetie."

I hung up again before he could answer. I had meant it, too. If Turricci was connected, that meant whoever killed my parents had underestimated them — and me.

The sun was setting by the time I wandered off the ferry onto Sicilian soil. Stepping foot on my ancestral land, I wondered why my parents had never taken us to Sicily.

Growing up, they had taken us everywhere in Italy *besides* Sicily. We'd spent months on the Cinque Terre, visited Rome half a dozen times, Florence, Venice, and Pompeii. But never Sicily.

Once I asked if we had any relatives in Sicily we could visit and my mother looked pained and left the room. My father told me that some memories were too difficult for my mother and it was best not to bring up Sicily again.

I wondered if it hurt too much for her because she had lost her parents at such a young age. She was only fifteen when they died.

Being in Sicily made me feel nervous and vulnerable. I needed some way to protect myself. Cab drivers knew everything. In San Francisco, they could tell you where to find prostitutes, heroin, or contraband. If they didn't know, they always knew someone who did.

Hitching my backpack over one shoulder, I hailed a cab and leaning in the window, asked if he knew where I could get a gun, a *pistola*. I flashed so many euro in front of him, he just nodded for me to get in.

He drove to a small shanty along the side of a hill overlooking rough seas. He told me I'd find what I needed inside.

I got out, leaned in and handed him the euro. I was about to tell him I'd pay him extra if he'd wait, but as soon as his chubby fist closed around the money, he roared off, nearly running over my sandaled foot. Motherfucker. I was stuck at some shack with some gun dealer, miles away from civilization. I hitched my bag on my shoulder, took a deep breath, and headed for the blue-painted door.

Before I could raise my hand to knock, the door flew open. A man in his twenties with an unbuttoned white shirt and thick hair waved back in a pompadour stood there, leering at me.

"*Voglio una pistola*." I want a gun. I didn't crack a smile.

He gestured for me to enter. A voice inside warned me to get the hell out of there. I looked around. In both directions lay an empty stretch of road. In the distance, far below, was the sea. We had passed one or two buildings on the drive. It would be a long, hot walk back.

I started to turn to leave, but then the man smiled.

"Come in. Are you hungry? We are about to eat." He spoke in Italian.

It sounded so normal, I smiled back, and despite my gut instinct, walked inside. A shiver ran across my arm as I stepped into the cooler, dim room that reeked of stale cigarette smoke. But beneath the smoke was the sweet smell I recognized from childhood – sauce simmering on the stove. It was familiar and comforting. Maybe this would be okay.

Once my eyes adjusted, I saw that the young man had left through a swinging door to what must have been a kitchen. The living room was small and tidy. Two love seats faced one another. An older man sat slumped on one.

"Sit." He said in Italian.

I perched on that edge, clutching my backpack with white knuckles. I eyed the door to the kitchen, but all was quiet.

"Why you need gun?" His English was rusty, but I could tell he was proud of it.

I shrugged.

The man, who had thin gray hair slicked back and a pressed light blue shirt sat up straighter, tapping an unlit cigarette on the couch. He raised his eyebrow. He wasn't taking my shrug for an answer.

"I'm an American woman in Sicily."

The man laughed and lit the cigarette, not taking his eyes off of me until he exhaled.

I set my backpack on the floor next to my feet and leaned back on the couch adopting the man's relaxed posture. He stared at me and I looked, unflinchingly, back.

He watched me for a few seconds and then nodded as if he had made up his mind. As if on cue, the younger man returned with a small pistol.

"You know how to work this?" He asked in Italian.

I eyed it. "Yep."

"One million euro." It was a fair price. Only about seven hundred dollars American.

I leaned down to grab my backpack at my feet. I'd moved some cash into it while I was in the cab so I didn't have to reveal my hidden money belt to the gun dealers. By the time I saw the man's pants leg inches away from my face, I knew I'd made a mistake. Then it all went black.

CHAPTER TWENTY-SIX

"YOU DON'T COME TO SICILY and ask to buy a gun." The voice, speaking in Italian, seemed to come from far away.

The words, followed by raucous laughter, dimly made their way into my throbbing head as my body tumbled downward, knocking against scratchy bushes, scraping sticks, and small rocks that felt like punches. I was afraid to open my eyes. I knew it was best to keep my eyes tightly closed. When I finally came to a painful stop, I slowly opened my eyes. All I saw was brilliant blue sky above me. I was stuck against a prickly bush that had stopped my rolling further down the steep hillside.

A bird whistled a happy song and I heard tires squealing from what sounded like far away. Gingerly, I sat up. I was near the bottom of a steep, weed and flowered-covered incline. A craggy outcrop of bushes and rocks had stopped my body from continuing its roll right off the cliff. I could hear the surf pounding some ways down the hill a few hundred feet below. So, despite appearances, I knew they didn't want me dead. I was certain if they had wanted me dead, they would've put a bullet in my head before sending my body plunging down the hill, or at the very least, waited around to make sure I went soaring off the cliff into the ocean.

My head throbbed where I'd been whacked with the pistol. I tried to stand, but felt dizzy and slumped back into a sitting position on a large rock, putting my head between my hands. Of course, they'd taken my backpack. I frantically patted under my jeans. My money belt was there. Thank God, they hadn't searched me.

They were just playing with me. Sending me a message. As far as I could tell the message was "Don't be a stupid American girl who thinks she can play with the big boys in Sicily."

I'd learned my lesson. The Tenderloin and Hunter's Point in San Francisco were Disneyland compared to Sicily.

The warrior learns from his mistakes and grows stronger, more powerful.

It took me a while to make it to the road I'd spotted. I headed to the right, which seemed to be north. I had traveled south to get to the shack.

My head hurt and as I walked, I daydreamed about coming across a small café where I could get a large glass of water and four aspirin. But the road, which was up against the side of the hill on one side and overlooking the ocean on the other, didn't seem to have any businesses. No cars, either.

After about thirty minutes, I heard the distant rumble of an engine and stepped to the shoulder of the road, ready to flag the driver down. The vehicle that rounded the bend was an old rusty pickup truck and the gray-haired driver didn't even slant his eyes my way as he passed despite my yells and frantic waving.

I kept walking.

It took me about another half hour to reach a small village.

When I saw the road leveling out and the line of small buildings in front of me, I wanted to cry with relief. Instead, I kept on, encouraged by the thought of aspirin and water.

It wasn't a store. It was a small cluster of homes. Nobody seemed to be at the first house, but my knock was answered at the second. A teenage girl looked at me as if she were bored.

"Do you have a phone?" I asked in Italian.

Instead of answering, she closed the door. I should have asked for water and aspirin. A few seconds later, she handed me a phone and stood there in the doorway watching me.

A half hour later, I'd downed some aspirin, drank a huge glass of water, and was waiting for a driver from a hotel in Taormina to pick me up. I knew after that blow to the head, I'd need a day or two to recover. It would drive me crazy. I had things to do. But I also knew my body needed some down time.

The clerk at the Grand Hotel Timeo in Taormina said they had a doctor on staff who could come look at my head. I said I'd pass. I'd had a concussion before, from getting a kick in the head during my Budo training. Only time would make it better.

CHAPTER TWENTY-SEVEN

THREE DAYS LATER, THE throbbing in my head had disappeared. I had taken it easy, lying in bed most of the day, watching TV and ordering room service for food and toiletries. The luxury hotel was ostentatious. The bathroom alone was nearly as big as my entire Tenderloin apartment.

I thought such a lazy lifestyle would've driven me crazy, but my body told me otherwise.

But this morning I woke up ready to go.

All my clothes had been in my backpack, so, dressed in the only clothes I had, which were smelly, dirty and ripped, I headed down to the fancy hotel's lobby. There, at a few of the expensive designer shops, I bought pink lacy lingerie, a black bikini, a burnt orange sundress, a cashmere wrap, black linen pants, four short-sleeve white T-shirts and four long-sleeve black T-shirts.

After a shower, I headed back downstairs to one of the hotel's restaurants. I gulped down eggs, bacon, and coffee and left the waiter a tip double the price of my meal. The waiter, who was in a tuxedo and very prim and proper, swooped up my euro without blinking. I took a chance and put my hand on his arm.

"*Scusi*," I said and asked him how to find the villa that belonged to my mother.

He said, sure, no problem, did I have the address?

I showed him the address on a piece of paper. I'd scribbled Turricci's name beside it. The waiter's eyes widened as he read it. Without answering, he walked away, jerking his arm out of my grasp.

I got the same response from the three cabbies I asked to take me to the address. The first one started sputtering in Italian, leaped out of his cab and closed the door I had opened. The second one just kept shaking his head and repeating "no." The third one sped away when I showed him the address.

Now I was really curious.

I FOUND A RENTAL CAR agency and paid cash to rent a small Fiat. It took me less than twenty minutes to find the villa. It stood alone on a bluff overlooking the ocean. The driveway led to a giant iron gate flanked by a huge stone wall that hugged the curves of the hills as far as the eye could see, all the way to what must have been the cliff overlooking the sea.

There was no buzzer at the gate. It was fortified like a castle. There was one way in – through that gate and I wasn't getting in unless I scaled it myself. For a half second I considered it. After all, it was *my* property now, right?

With all the windows of the Fiat down, I drove away, trying to come up with a plan, inhaling the peculiar combination of scents that made up Sicily — some intoxicating mix of salty air, lemons, and Jasmine.

Soon I came upon the nearest town, if it could be called that — basically a blip on a lonely stretch of rural road. The café was a tiny room at the front of a cottage with iron café tables and chairs outside. Two older men sat drinking espressos and playing some board game I didn't recognize.

One winked at me when I walked past. Inside, a small bar stretched across one side of the room. An ancient but sturdy espresso machine took up most of the bar. There was no menu. An older man with a generous head of silver hair and equally generous belly smiled when I walked in.

I ordered an espresso before I brought up the villa. The man stepped back and squinted at me.

"Bonadonna?"

My mother's maiden name. I knew I didn't look anything like my mother, who had blonde hair and brown eyes.

"*Si. La mia madre.*"

The man made the sign of the cross. He knew she was dead.

"How do you know?"

"We know what happens to the people from our village."

Then he came out from behind the bar and with a heavy sigh, sat down at a table and patted the chair beside him.

I carried my espresso over and sat down, wondering why he looked so sad.

I explained in Italian that I was trying to find someone who could let me into the villa.

The man shook his head.

I took the deeds out of my bag and handed them to the man. He barely glanced at them, as if he knew what they said. He waved his hand. And told me in Italian to go home and keep the past buried from the light. I was confused. Wasn't that what Mrs. Gutmann had said?

"I need to speak to Mr. Turricci. Where can I find him? I need to talk to him. I came all the way from America to tell him some news about my mother."

This time there was no mistaking the fear in his eyes. He didn't answer. He put the broom in a corner and walked out, into another room without saying a word. After about ten minutes when it was clear he wasn't going to return, I made myself comfortable. I could outwait him. An hour later, the door opened. The man handed me a slip of paper. It said: "Boat. Lucia-Grazia. Messina Harbor." A boat with my mother's name?

"You no get this from me. I want to live a nice old age." His English was rusty, but he made his point.

"I've never seen you before in my life." I said, and gave him a long, slow wink. He didn't smile. He shook his head sadly and walked me to the door. I heard the lock turn behind me.

Night was falling in indigos and purples before me as I walked down the dock to the Lucia-Grazia. I'd changed into the black linen pants and a black T-shirt and pulled my hair back in a low ponytail. I took a roundabout way, going first to an adjacent dock to scope it out. The Lucia-Grazia was not a boat. It was a yacht.

The windows were dark. But then I noticed a tiny glow. Somebody on the deck was smoking. I crouched down. I wanted to get on that yacht. A little way down, a small walkway connected the two docks. I could make it to the yacht in ten minutes.

I waited. The only sounds were waves lapping up on the dock and the distant sounds of people having a party on another boat. I was having trouble keeping my eyes open when I finally saw the tiny glow of a cigarette moving toward the front of the yacht. I squinted my eyes a bit. Whoever it was, the person was getting off the boat. A dark beefy figure made its way down the dock toward the shore. I leaped to my feet and ran until I was in front of the yacht. It was at least three stories tall. I only hesitated for a moment before I raced up the gangplank and leaped over the small chain. I headed for the front of the yacht, the farthest away from the dock, and went up one level. Most of the second level consisted of a deck with teakwood chairs and tables. With a shaking hand, I tugged on a sliding glass door that easily slid open. It led to a circular room with curved white couches surrounding a giant round glass coffee table with a fresh flower bouquet and a Ming vase.

The circle room led to a giant dining room. Moonlight streaked in through the glass walls, illuminating the scene. A large table was set for eight underneath a Joan Miró painting. Off to one side was a white baby grand piano. Next to that, an entire small wall was set up as a bar with a mirror reflecting the colors of the bottles. I poured myself a shot of bourbon and gulped it down in two sips. Then downed another to stop my hands from shaking so much. I carefully wiped the rim of the glass and put it back on its mirrored tray.

A small circular staircase led to the master bedroom. The entire roof of the master bedroom was a domed skylight, giving a glimpse of a dark, star-spotted night and letting in moonlight bright enough for me to see. A red silk duvet covered the bed. A large dark wood dresser had an assortment of gold and diamond cufflinks resting on a gold tray and nothing else. Tucking my hands into my long sleeves to hide my fingerprints, I opened every drawer on the giant dresser. Nothing but clothes, silk pajamas, silk shirts and even silk boxers. I also rifled through the closet — designer men's clothes reeking of cologne. I pushed the clothes to one side looking for a safe or hidden panel but didn't see anything unusual. I peeked behind the paintings — this time a Picasso and a Monet — but only found blank wall.

Voices and a rumbling sent me scurrying. The engines on the yacht had started. Lights flickered on around the boat, including in the master bedroom. I darted toward a sliding glass door, which led to a giant enclosed deck overlooking the rest of the yacht. I stood against the edge and peered over. I didn't see a soul.

The master bedroom held two other doors. The first was a bathroom. The second was a connecting door to an office.

Quickly, I yanked open the roll-top desk. Nothing but a quill pen with a real ink pot and some thick, expensive feeling stationary embossed in gold with the initials S.A.T.

The top drawer of the desk held a flask and more office supplies. The bottom drawer was filled with files. My fingers tripped through them. Each file folder was labeled. The names meant nothing to me—Carlton Ltd. Sardinia house. Jasmine Corp.

Then, my heart stopped. Bay View.

I grabbed it and quickly flicked it open. It was a contract for the Bay View Development. Turricci was going to pay Vito two hundred and fifty million dollars for the mixed-use center when it was developed.

San Francisco had one of the most inflated real estate markets in the country, but this seemed excessive. Turricci wasn't even buying the land. The contract was for him to buy the developed property. Sure, it was a luxury development, but there were dozens of them in the city.

Well, if I was looking for motive, I'd found it.

Without my father standing in the way of the development, Vito could proceed and stood to make two hundred and fifty million dollars.

A noise in the hall sent my heart into my throat. When the doorknob leading to the hall turned, I shoved the file folder back in the drawer and raced back into the master bedroom just in time to see the door handle turn.

CHAPTER TWENTY-EIGHT

I HAD JUST ENOUGH TIME to drop and roll under the massive king bed before the door opened.

Luckily, whomever owned the Yeti-sized feet only walked briefly through the room and out again.

But I was terrified to move.

The warrior has cultivated patience. The ability to watch and wait is essential to be effective in battle.

I only dared crawl out hours later when the yacht's engine finally quieted. Peeking outside the window, I saw we were back where we started.

I watched two men go down the gangplank and waited for them to hit the dry land before I made a mad dash for the dock.

Fifteen minutes later, I was back at my hotel. I ordered a massive plate of bacon and eggs and toast and took a long bubble bath in the sunken tub with the view of the sea. When I was done, I crawled into bed and slept until dark.

After a shower, I decided I needed a drink. And I wanted to have sex. Badly. I'd had erotic dreams about Bobby all day long. In the shower, I'd thought about him and ran my soapy hands over my body until it had made me weak with desire. I knew better than to ever see him again. It was way too dangerous, but I couldn't deny that he had cast some wicked spell on me.

Down at the hotel bar, I paused in the doorway. The bar had lots of business travelers, apparently. Large groups of boisterous men speaking English occupied most of the tables. I walked past them all. The last thing I wanted was to sleep with an American man in Italy.

A sultry Italian voice caught my ear. I turned slowly. At the end of the bar a man with perfect gray hair and an Armani suit in nearly the same color looked as if he owned the place. His black eyes met mine. He gave me a long, slow smile and raised an eyebrow. I headed his way.

When I reached the seat near his, a glass of *Veuve Clicquot* champagne was waiting for me, sparkling in the soft light from the chandeliers hanging throughout the bar.

"Is there something to celebrate?" I asked, sliding onto the stool without taking my eyes off him.

"Most certainly." He raised his glass to mine. "Our meeting here tonight."

I couldn't hide the small smile that crept onto my face as I raised my own glass to his. "Salut."

Two glasses later, we were out by the pool.

"Tell me about yourself, Gia," he said, his black eyes boring into mine.

Had I told him my name? His attention was intoxicating. It was as if every word I said mesmerized him and he couldn't stop looking at me. But he was keeping his distance. When I scooted closer to him, he'd adjusted himself slightly.

I'd come down to the bar to get laid and he was making it difficult.

"Gia. Do you know how beautiful you are?"

I smiled. But a small part of me was suspicious. If he thought I was so beautiful why was he so standoffish?

"I want to know everything about you, Gia Valentina Santella." For a second, I paused. Had his voice sounded snide when he said my last name? I looked up at him sharply and he smiled. I must have imagined it.

I instantly regretted telling him my full name. Stupid rookie mistake. I knew better. Usually with one-night stands I used a made-up name.

"Gia. You have much sadness in you." He sighed. "I wish I could make it all go away."

I looked away. This was definitely not going as planned. I wanted sex. Not a fucking romance. I'd give it one more shot.

"I'm cold." I said, pretending to shiver.

He understood and within a minute was leading me by the hand to the elevator outside the bar. Once inside, he inserted a special key into the slot marked "P." Penthouse. As the elevator door opened onto a completely glass walled suite with views of the sea in all directions, I wondered again, who *was* this man? Maybe he did own the hotel.

He stood at an elaborate mirrored bar, fixing us drinks. When he handed me mine, I closed my fingers around his.

He closed his eyes for a second and looked uncomfortable.

My God. What was going on?

"I thought we could talk more. You could tell me about your life in Monterey."

For a second I froze. I didn't remember mentioning my hometown. I was drunk, but I was always careful about revealing personal details. But then again, I thought, as my vision blurred, I'd also told him my full name, hadn't I?"

I leaned my head back and looked at his lips. "I don't want to talk." I slurred the words and then pressed my lips against his neck. I pressed my body against his and could feel him respond. A guttural moan escaped from his body and then he pulled back violently.

Before I realized it, he had his arm on mine and had led me back to my own room. I didn't remember telling him what room I was in. He reached into my bag, withdrew my key card and opened my door.

"Will you be okay?"

"Fine." I said curtly. I was pissed. I'd never been turned down before.

"I'd like to have breakfast with you. I'll send for you at ten, give you plenty of time to sleep this off. There is something I want to discuss with you."

After my door closed, I drank four giant glasses of water, took four aspirin and set my alarm for eight. I had no intention of having breakfast with that man. I didn't care what he wanted to discuss. It was then I realized he had never told me his name.

The next morning, I quickly packed and then headed downstairs to check out. My plane left from Rome in twelve hours. I had my proof. It was time to act on it.

CHAPTER TWENTY-NINE

I DON'T KNOW WHO WAS happier to see me once I got back to San Francisco, Django or Thanh-Thanh. She kept squeezing my elbow and speaking to me in Vietnamese. I didn't know what she was saying. I hoped she wasn't telling me that watching Django had been a pain in the butt.

I'd bought her an assortment of scarves and perfumes and even a silk robe and slippers at the duty-free shop at the Rome airport. I was lucky to have her help with my dog. I handed her three hundred dollars. She shook her head, but I pointed at Django, miming her walking him. She shook her head again, but I held the money to my heart in a begging gesture and she actually rolled her eyes and then took it, giving me a small bow.

Inside my apartment, I collapsed on my bed, exhausted from jet lag and ready to sleep for the rest of the day. Django jumped up on the bed, licked my face and then settled down beside me to take a nap.

When I woke, it was dark and I was starving.

I grabbed Django's leash, and put my gun in its holster under my big Army coat. Django skipped around in frenetic circles until I clipped on his leash and opened the door.

Downstairs, Ethel wasn't in her usual spot. I hadn't seen her earlier, either. Maybe she'd already headed for the church early to sleep.

Grabbing a burner cell phone out of my bag, I dialed Susie's parents' house in Berkeley. Her mother immediately put Susie on the line.

"Oh, Gia, we were worried about you," she said.

"Me? I'm fine. How's Kato?"

"Much better. He's sleeping right now or I'd let you talk to him. He's a bit more tired than usual and keeps complaining that we won't let him go back to his dojo and are making him relax for another few days."

"It'll be good for him," I said. "How's his head?"

"The doctor said he might have some memory issues and fuzzy thinking for a few months, but there's no permanent damage."

"Thank God," I breathed the words out in a big sigh. Django stopped to do his business and I dug around in my purse for a plastic baggie.

"Gia, we're worried about you, though. Kato said these guys weren't messing around. They wanted to know where you were ..."

"Yeah, I'm going to take care of that. Why don't you guys stay there a bit longer?" I eyed a guy walking on the opposite site of the street. He had baggy pants and a big coat and looked like he was about to head my way. I turned slightly and pulled back my jacket so the streetlight glinted on the handle of my gun. The man headed in the other direction.

"Gia, be careful. Kato said if some of his students hadn't arrived early, he's pretty sure those men would've killed him." Her voice was quiet.

I swallowed hard. "I know. You just stay safe with the boys and Kato. I'll call you in the next day or two. It should all be over by then."

I hung up before she could answer.

When I got to Club Katrina, I realized I probably wouldn't be able to bring Django inside so I kept walking until I got to a hoagie shop. Wasn't my first choice, but it was an easy place to tie Django up in front of while I ordered. I got a plain roast beef for Django and a Spicy Italian sub for me.

I brought our dinners back to my apartment and started to make plans. Armed with the information I'd found in Italy, I knew it was time to confront Vito.

I'd head down to Monterey tomorrow. Kato and his family needed to get back to their normal lives. The time for gathering evidence against my godfather had passed. I wasn't going to need any more proof. Instead, I'd get a confession. My godfather had killed my parents and I was going to make him tell me why he did it. He would confess to me that he was a greedy bastard. He would beg my forgiveness. And then I would kill him.

CHAPTER THIRTY

MAKING MY WAY STEALTHILY by the golden glow of street lights filtering in the windows, I crawled onto the bed and held the long knife to my godfather's wrinkled throat.

The covers were neatly pulled up to his chest. His wheelchair parked nearby. I straddled his body, my knees pinning his arms, and dipped my head close to his. His eyes fluttered open and he tried to raise his arms to his throat. His eyes focused on me in the dim light.

"Gia?" He genuinely seemed confused but stopped struggling.

"Don't act innocent with me, Vito. It's time you paid for your sins."

"What?" His eyes blinked rapidly.

"You killed my parents. You killed my brother. You sent those goons to kill me. And you beat up, Kato."

"No, no. I swear." He tried to shake his head but the pressure of the knife stopped him.

"Bullshit." I let the knife press just a little bit harder. "I'm here to avenge my mother and father, Vito. You know I have to do this. You know it's my duty as a daughter."

My hands were steady. My voice even. My heart rate slow and steady. I'd thrown up twice on the drive down to Monterey, but now, with the knife pressed against Vito's saggy neck, a cool calmness had settled upon me. I nestled the knife between two floppy folds of skin. I could tell from the shimmer of fear in his eyes, he knew then that he would die at my hands. He struggled to sit up, but I put more pressure on his arms and chest.

"You sent those men to kill me. You ruined my father's business and you were trying to save yourself with the Bay View deal. I know everything."

"The men I sent," he said, struggling to speak. "Those men were to protect you. I've been looking for you. Your life is in danger."

"You killed my mother and father. They loved you!" I was crying now.

"I didn't kill your parents. They died in a fire, Gia, you know that."

"I don't know that!" My words seethed from my mouth with a hissing noise. What he didn't say spoke volumes. He didn't deny the other deaths.

"*Your* men killed Christopher. *Your* men beat up, Kato. On your orders! Go ahead and deny it and I'll end it right now." I said, pushing the knife harder until a tiny bit of blood appeared along its edge.

The warrior knows his enemies will deny all until the death. But the warrior must stay true to his course.

His eyes grew hard. He didn't say a word.

I leaned down in his face. "What did Kato ever do to you? He could have died from that attack."

"I needed to find you."

"So, you could kill me, too?"

"No, to protect you."

"I'm not stupid, Vito. You killed my brother and nearly beat my friend Kato to death and yet you look me in the eyes and say you didn't kill my parents and haven't tried to kill me? How do you expect me to believe this?"

The sound of glass breaking in the other room made me jerk back. The knife sliced my finger slightly and a large drop of blood dripped onto my godfather's pajama collar. The sounds of a struggle and a startling scream broke the silence.

Vito grabbed my wrist. Not to take away the knife but to pull my head close to his ear. "They're here," he whispered. "They must've followed you. Go, run."

I stopped, stunned. Was it a trick? Had he been telling the truth this whole time?

"Go, on your mother's soul, I beg you to run."

His eyes were wild. He was afraid.

I ran.

I slipped out the bedroom window and ran for the fence. I scaled it in one fluid movement and ran, cutting through backyards and not stopping until I'd reached the Carmel Mission.

I ducked into the ancient church, kneeling in the last row of pews, trying to catch my breath and make sense of what had just happened. It wasn't until I heard the cacophony of sirens, police and ambulance and fire trucks, that I knew.

My godfather was dead.

CHAPTER THIRTY-ONE

I CURLED UP IN A PEW in the candlelit mission and waited for morning to come. I still needed to figure out how to get back to San Francisco. The rental car, parked back near my godfather's house, was a loss. I thought again of the cars in my parents' garage but if what my godfather said was true—that someone else out there wanted me dead—my parents' house was an obvious place to look. I didn't even know where to start. I'd been convinced that my godfather was the killer, but now it looked like someone else was on the scene. I supposed there was a chance my godfather was lying and that one of his many enemies had broken into his house to kill him and it had nothing to do with me.

I didn't think my family had any enemies. If my godfather had really sent those men to protect me and bring me back to Monterey, that still didn't explain why would someone kill my parents and then try to kill me?

What I did know was that I'd have to figure out some other way to get back home. I didn't dare go to Dante's mother's house again. Before, when I thought it was my godfather who wanted me dead, I hadn't worried about her safety. But with this new information — all bets were off. I couldn't take the chance of putting anyone else in danger. Not after what happened to Kato.

I curled up on a back pew. The mission bells ringing at eight woke me. The church around me was filled with tourists who had just got off a tour bus and were loudly commenting on the beautiful sacristy. With my coat pulled over my head, they'd probably thought I was a vagrant. I felt like one.

After tidying up a bit in one of the bathrooms at the mission, I snuck onto one of the empty tour buses parked out front. I waited to make my move until I saw a driver pull out a pack of smokes and sneak around the backside of the bus. I didn't care where it was headed as long as it was far away from here. I sat in a row toward the back and buried my face in a brochure about the Mission when people started boarding the bus. When the bus started up, a couple of elderly ladies kept looking at me and whispering. I closed my eyes and pretended to sleep. I figured I'd probably taken one of their seats.

It wasn't until the bus pulled over for a snack break at a coffee shop in Salinas and all of the passengers had filed out except me, that the tour guide noticed me.

"Excuse me. I don't recall you being on the bus before." The woman's neat bun and the frown between her eyes meant no nonsense. "This tour is for the Women's Club of Gilroy."

I acted shocked and jumped out of my seat, grabbing my bag. "Oh, my gosh, I had a migraine and must've crawled on the wrong bus and fallen asleep. I can't believe I got on the wrong one. Oh no!"

I acted so distraught, she believed me. I rushed past her. "I need to find a phone. My friends are going to be worried sick."

I rented a car in Salinas under another fake identity Darling had given me.

Back in San Francisco, I dropped off the rental car and took a cab back to the Tenderloin. As I paid the cabbie, I looked around again for Ethel. I hadn't seen her since before I left for Europe. I hoped she was okay and not passed out drunk in some alley. Her absence worried me. I'd lost too many people around me not to worry.

When I finally made it to my room and gave Django enough pets for him to settle down, I curled up in my bed with all my clothes on and just stared at the wall. Now that I was safe and could relax, the implications of the day before struck me full force.

My godfather was dead. Although I had just settled under the covers, I leaped out of bed, got a chair so I could reach my mother's box from its high shelf in my kitchen area.

The answer had to be in there somewhere.

I reached for the box and felt empty air.

My hand ran over the shelf again. There it was, pushed farther back than I had thought.

I opened a can of tuna and shared it with Django as I sorted through a stack of love letters from my dad. I read about six of them and my heart both hurt and filled with happiness at the love my parents had shared.

From what I could piece together, my mother and father had started dating when they were fourteen years old. When my father turned sixteen, he left Sicily and came to Monterey to work for his father on a fishing boat. The two teens pledged their eternal love for one another and made plans to marry once my mother turned eighteen. Then the letters grew sad. My mother's parents were both killed in a freak boat wreck on their way to Sardinia.

"My love. I am so lost. The pain is almost too much to bear. When I think about mama and papa, the world around me turns black. If I didn't have you, I would just walk off the cliff by my house. Thoughts of you are the only thing that stop me from doing that."

I stopped reading for a second. I was living my mother's life. We were both orphans who had lost everything. Except, unlike her, I had no boyfriend. I had no one to love. My world had been black since their death.

Even though she always loved Christopher more, even though I always felt second best, her absence left a hole in my heart. And I knew no man would ever love me as much as my father had loved me.

My father wrote back begging her to be patient and to wait for him. He even offered to come back to Sicily and get her as soon as he had saved enough money.

The next letter my mother wrote sounded a bit more upbeat. She had been taken in by a friend of the family she called Uncle Tony.

I paused on that name. Uncle Tony was Mateo Antonio Turricci. I'd bet on it. I read on. He had become her guardian. That must be why he gave her that villa and the surrounding land. That explained the connection between Vito and Turricci—they knew each other from the old country. But it still didn't explain why Turricci was going to pay Vito an insane amount of money for a development worth one-fourth of that.

CHAPTER THIRTY-TWO

I SNUGGLED WITH DJANGO and slept for two days until my jet-lag had worn off and I felt like myself again. My head still hurt occasionally and my body was covered in cuts and bruises from being tossed around like a rag doll, but I'd felt worse.

On the third morning, I made a strong cup of espresso, tugged on some faded jeans and an old sweater and headed for the door with Django practically bouncing at my heels. I wanted to go visit Jessica Stark. The contract I'd seen in Italy still stumped me. Maybe Jessica Stark knew why Turricci was so interested in the land.

Outside the building, I glanced again at the spot where Ethel usually sat during the day. The flattened cardboard boxes she sat on were still there. I made a note to ask Thanh-Thanh about Ethel.

THE CANCER HAD DONE a number on Jessica Stark. Large shadows pooled under her eyes and her cheekbones were sharp slices slanting up to her hairline. The smile she gave me was wan. Death was shadowing her every move.

She didn't seem surprised to see me. She held up a rocks glass to toast me and shrugged.

"I figure there's no reason to wait until noon anymore."

I pressed my lips together. When she poured me a drink, I clinked my glass to hers and downed it in one gulp.

"I came to tell you that you don't have to worry anymore. My godfather's dead."

Her shrill laughter startled me.

"It's too late. I went to the oncologist yesterday. It's spread to my brain. It's a matter of days. Maybe hours."

I looked down. "I'm sorry."

She shrugged.

I felt bad grilling a dying woman for information, but I needed to know.

"Jessica, can you think of any reason why an investor would pay two hundred and fifty million for this development? I mean, is there a gold vein buried underground or what?"

She frowned and her eyebrows knit together. "That's how much your lying greedy godfather was getting for these digs?"

"Can you think of any reason someone would pay that much?"

She hiccupped. "Not a clue."

I sighed. "Me, either."

Grabbing my bag, I headed toward to door.

"I'm sorry to have bothered you. Again."

"How about keeping a dying woman company?" She held up a bottle of gin.

"When you put it that way, it's an offer I can't refuse."

She laughed. "Come on, stay a while. Want to watch a movie?"

"Sure, why the hell not."

We sat, slumped on the couch drinking gin and howling with laughter at *The Big Lebowski*. When I heard her snoring softly beside me, I covered her with a throw blanket, lowered the volume of the TV, and crept out.

It was the last time I saw Jessica Stark.

ON MY WAY HOME, I SAW a stand with flowers for sale. Dozens of red roses. I thought about Ethel. That fuck of a husband had beat her nearly to death and then thought he could buy her roses and that would make everything okay.

Well, it didn't. I was glad he was dead. For a second, I thought about buying Ethel roses. Just for the hell of it. To show that someone could be kind to her for no reason, not as a way to make up for nearly beating her to death. But I didn't know how she would take it. I would never forgive myself if it brought up bad memories. I'd ask her. I'd ask if it'd be okay if I bought her some roses one day because she deserved something pretty.

When I got home, I knocked on Thanh-Thanh's door. Through a series of hand gestures and broken English, I asked about Ethel. From the older woman's responses, she hadn't seen Ethel around for days. Downstairs, I knocked on Trang's door.

He opened it up and yawned.

"I ain't seen the old biddy for a while."

Oh, my God. My heart pounded in my throat.

I waited until eight thirty at night and headed for Saint Boniface. I'd heard that doors to the church closed for the night at nine. The pews were already filled. I began at the altar and slowly walked down the aisle softly calling Ethel's name. A couple of people swore at me, but nobody answered my call. I looked for a head wrapped in a paisley scarf. About half way down the aisle, a man with a bald head and long beard sat up. "Ethel ain't been around for long time."

"You know where she's staying?"

He shook his head and laid back down, pulling a dingy brown blanket up to his nose.

THE NEXT MORNING, I did a short Budo workout in my place to get back in the swing of things. Then, dressed as demurely as I could manage— flat shoes, my hair back in a sleek ponytail, and big black sunglasses—I headed to the police station.

At the front desk, I said my elderly aunt was homeless and missing and I was concerned.

After I filled out a missing report, I asked the clerk how soon I might know something. He shrugged. He gestured toward a bulletin board on the way out. "We'll put a missing person poster up there. You can check back tomorrow."

I glared at him. He was useless.

"I need answers now. She's never just disappeared like this." It wasn't really true since I barely knew her, but I wanted him to take me seriously. I had a really bad feeling about Ethel's disappearance.

I'd turned to walk out when the clerk called after me, "You checked the morgue?"

I didn't respond. On my way out, my heart stopped for a minute as I passed a bulletin board plastered with wanted and missing person's posters. My face and name were on one poster. I didn't stop to read why. Blood pounded in my ears but I managed not to break stride as I casually walked out the double doors.

Outside, I leaned against the wall, breathing heavily. What the fuck? Had my godfather lied and reported me for committing some nonexistent crime? He must have been really desperate to find me. It wasn't a "Missing Person" poster—it was a "Wanted" poster.

Just in case, I kept my sunglasses on when I walked into the morgue about twenty minutes later.

"I don't have an Ethel Swanson, but we've got some unidentified," the clerk there told me. "Can you be more specific?"

"Older black lady maybe in her sixties with short gray hair. She usually wears a scarf around her head. Homeless?" I knew it wasn't much.

"Your aunt, huh?"

"Yep." I looked her dead in the eye.

The clerk looked away and scrolled through her computer screen. "I got one that fits that description," she said.

My heart stopped.

"Does she have any identifying marks? Tattoos, special dental work, anything like that?" The clerk asked.

I shook my head sadly. I didn't know.

"What about something she might have had on her person, like a handbag or something?"

The flask.

"A silver flask with the initials GVS."

"Hold." She got up and went out a door.

She came back with a plastic bag. "This one?"

Good God. Inside was my flask.

A wave of sadness rolled across my body. Thoughts of her dying cold and alone in some alley maybe from alcohol poisoning. A thought horrified me — what if that night we had drank that booze and smoked that weed, what if that had done her in? What if that had been too much and she had died from it?

"How did she die?" My voice, barely above a whisper, cracked.

"You'll have to talk to the police department."

I scrunched up my face in confusion. "I was just there. They didn't say shit."

The woman seemed to take pity on me. "If you were there filing a missing person report earlier, they might not have made the connection yet. Go back and talk to them. But don't expect much because it's an open case and they won't be able to tell you much."

"I don't understand."

She looked over her glasses at me. "I'm sorry to tell you this about your aunt. Her death was ruled a homicide."

CHAPTER THIRTY-THREE

EVEN THOUGH IT SEEMED like every person I had a conversation with ended up dead, it didn't dawn on me that Ethel's murder was connected to me until I was nearly home. I smelled something odd in the air and then, still six blocks away, saw the plumes of smoke billowing into the sky.

Two block away I began running.

My entire block was lined with fire trucks and emergency vehicles.

In front of my building, three giant fire engines were parked and firemen stood on tall ladders shooting water out of hoses. Two ambulances were parked nearby.

A crowd was gathered across the street from my building. Smoke poured from the top floor and flames licked out of the windows. Django and Thanh-Thanh.

I raced toward the police tape and was stopped by strong arms.

It was just like in the movies — a screaming hysterical woman being held back by a firefighter as she tried to fight her way into the burning building.

"Please! You have to help me. I live here. Is there anybody still in the building?" I was wild-eyed and my voice was shrill, but the man looked me in the eyes so calmly, I felt tension ease from my body for just a second. But then I began fighting again.

"We're trying to determine that right now," he said. "Wait over there. Our public information officer is gathering some details and will share them as soon as she can."

I walked closer in a daze, staying away from the small crowd of spectators. I slumped onto the curb and stared at a small pile of cigarette butts swirling in a bit of wind.

There was no hiding from it. People were dying because of me. If Ethel had been murdered like the woman said, it had to be because of me. It was my fault. I knew it in my bones.

There was no avoiding it. Thanh-Thanh. Trang. And that poor damn dog. I was trying to save him from an asshole master and instead sent him to a painful death.

I watched as firefighters rushed out of the building. I heard a familiar bark and raised my head. Django. And Thanh-Thanh on the other end of the leash. She was frowning as she watched the building. Relief shot through me.

I whistled and Thanh-Thanh's face lit up in a smile. How could she smile? She was homeless. Probably everything she owned was destroyed. But she raced over with short, waddling steps and embraced me, talking rapidly in Vietnamese. By her gestures, I figured out that Thanh-Thanh had taken Django for a walk so they'd been gone when the fire started. Thank God.

Django wasn't interested in me scratching his belly. His ears were up and his eyes on the building. Small whining sounds came rumbling from his throat.

After a few minutes, a small crowd began to gather a fireman with a clipboard. Thanh-Thanh and I walked over. The fire man gave us the details.

Nobody died in the fire.

Trang had kept the building up to code and had smoke alarms installed in every apartment and in the hallway on every floor. Thank

God. Then the fire captain said that it was arson. Somebody had set fire to the top floor apartment — mine.

They were investigating, but it was clear the fire was not accidental.

I was relieved nobody was injured or killed, but sickened that all these people had lost their homes. It was my fault. It was catastrophic for them. Unlike me, they'd lost all their material goods in the world. I'd always had something to fall back on. In a bank account.

I watched small groups huddling and crying. Red Cross workers showed up to pass out cards and tell all my neighbors — about a dozen lived in the six apartments — where they could sleep. These people had lost everything they owned. The fire captain said later, once the building was secured, firefighters would either let residents in to recover belongings or bring out any remaining possessions themselves for residents to sift through.

One thing was clear: Whoever was trying to kill me knew I was still in San Francisco.

I could easily buy more clothes and belongings. I had my gun. I could replace everything. Except one thing: The box that had belonged to my mother.

Those love letters my parents had exchanged seemed like my last link to them on this earth. And now they were gone. I had no home. No money. No nothing.

It seemed like it could get no worse.

A police car came to a screech with a dark sedan on its tail. Good. I hoped they had a lead on the arsonist. Because obviously, that was who was trying to kill me. Took them long enough to get here, though. Like the arsonist would be standing around.

"Little bit late to be in a hurry," I said, looking up at the smoldering remains of my building. It was still standing, but probably everything inside had been destroyed. I'm sure the building would have to be gutted.

I didn't notice the commotion that started in the crowd until some shiny black shoes were on the pavement in front of me and Django.

"Gia Santella?"

I looked up, warily.

"Monterey P.D. You're going to have to come with us. You're under arrest for the murder of Vittorio Guidi."

CHAPTER THIRTY-FOUR

I ACTUALLY LAUGHED. Until they jerked my arms behind my back and patted me down.

My gun.

"Weapon!"

"Don't move."

"Get down on the ground!"

The next thing I knew I was flat on the pavement with my cheek pressed up against a dirty cigarette butt. That was going to leave a mark.

"Get on the ground!" the cop said again.

I didn't think it was worth telling him I already was on the ground. If I got any closer, I'd be underground. My view was of feet. Lots of black shoes surrounding me. The ground reeked of piss and vomit and god knows what else. I gagged a little.

After a patting down that felt like a pummeling. I was yanked up by the cuffs, which dug painfully into my wrists and practically pushed to the unmarked car.

Thanh-Thanh met my eyes as I passed. I gave her a meaningful look up toward what remained of my apartment. She nodded. If anything had survived, which I doubted, she'd find it.

They threw me into the back of the squad car without reading me my Miranda rights. I sat there and wondered if I was really under arrest or they were just bullying me into a trip to Monterey for questioning.

I pressed my face against the cool glass of the window, taking in the night as we made the drive to Monterey. There was no way they had anything on me, so I doubted I could be under arrest. Could cops lie about something like that to get someone to give a confession? I wasn't sure. Then again, who knew how far the reach of my enemies spanned.

I knew, or at least believed, they could never pin Vito's death on me. They were chasing ghosts and soon they'd have to let me go. There was no way they could have anything on me. I mean, yeah, I was there that night, but that's it.

Then a chill ran across my scalp. I'd cut myself when I'd held the knife to his throat that night. My blood was at the murder scene.

CHAPTER THIRTY-FIVE

I'D THOUGHT UNDRESSING in the high school locker room every day in front of all the WASPy girls who called me names would be the most humiliating era of my life, but the body cavity search before they put me in a jail cell was right up there.

The orange jumpsuit they gave me was too small and rode uncomfortably up my crotch and stretched obscenely across my chest. I tried to tell the lady I wasn't a small, but a medium, and she pretended like she was deaf, turning her back on me until the guard prodded me from behind.

The fingerprints and mug shots weren't as bad as I thought. I couldn't decide whether to look tough or smirk. Sitting in a small holding cell waiting for someone to come get me to take me to my jail cell, I knew that even considering how to pose for a mug shot was deranged. I wasn't taking any of this very seriously. Maybe something was very wrong with me. Was I in shock? All I knew was that I couldn't wrap my head around the idea that I was under arrest.

But that drop of blood. Remembering it made my stomach flip flop. They'd need more than that. I'd just tell them exactly what happened. I started laughing hysterically. Exactly what happened? That I'd gone there with the intent of killing Vito but was scared off by the real killer? I definitely was losing it.

Before they took me to my cell, they gave me my one call.

Sal, Vito's attorney, sounded sleepy when he picked up. It was eleven at night.

"It's Gia. I'm in county. They say I killed Vito. But I didn't."

He gave a long sigh. "I'm in Bodega Bay. I'll be down first thing in the morning."

My small jail cell had a metal bed, a thin mattress, no pillow, and a toilet without a lid. No toilet paper. I banged on the bars to get someone, but my rattling went unanswered. The woman in the cell beside me mumbled something that sounded like "shut the fuck up" and "I'm gonna cut your tit off in the shower tomorrow morning." One or the other. Or both. Rather than answer, I curled up on the bed, which probably would give me bed bugs, crabs, and scabies in one fell swoop, and tried to sleep.

IN THE MORNING, THE guard brought me to a small visitor room. I looked around for cameras or recording devices before I even met Sal's eyes.

"Don't worry," Sal said, noting my glance around the room. "This is all privileged. No wires here."

He was dressed in a three-piece suit perfectly tailored to his tiny frame. His black hair was slicked back like an Italian film star. His shoes gleamed in the overhead light and his buffed nails did, too. I'd never had nails that looked that good in my life.

I hugged him. His body was stiff and awkward as if he couldn't wait for the hug to end. I immediately drew back and pulled up a chair.

"They're going to charge you with murder one. Any reason they might think you did it?" His tone was casual, but firm.

"Yeah. Because I actually went there to kill him, left a huge drop of my blood on his pajamas and then ran away before the killer got to him." It all came out in a rush. When I was done, I bit my lip and tried not to cry. Saying it out loud made it all real. I was fucked. I'd spend the rest of my life in prison.

"Back up a little, Gia. Last time I saw you, Vito had just given you your Ferrari and you were proclaiming your love for him to the heavens, asking if he would be your new father since your own dear dad was dead."

"Yeah. Well, things changed."

I spent the rest of the time filling Sal in on what had happened, starting with the letter from the forensic pathologist's wife. Sal, a life-long Catholic, paused from his note taking to make the sign of the cross whenever I mentioned any of the dead's names.

When I was done, I stared at the scummy, jail-issue slippers I was wearing. When Sal didn't say anything, I looked up. Hi face remained expressionless. The silence seemed roaring. Finally, he cleared his throat.

"Gia, how long have you known me?"

I shrugged.

"Let me put this another way. Gia, how old are you?"

"Twenty-three?" I said it like a question.

"So, we've known each other for twenty-three years. I was at your baptism and pretty much every big event in your life." He paused and looked me in the eye. "Is there any reason why you didn't come to me with all this?"

I swallowed hard and nodded. "I didn't know who I could trust." My voice was small and quiet and a bit ashamed.

He clamped his lips tightly together and nodded his head. "Okay. I get that. But now you have to trust me."

I nodded.

He told me he'd try to get me out on bail during my arraignment tomorrow and for me to hang in there.

Right before the guard took me away, Sal gave me a serious look.

"Spend the next twenty-four hours wisely. I want you to let all those pieces of information you've gathered, whether they are in your conscious or subconscious — put your brain to work and try to figure out who is behind all of this. I think you know who it is somewhere in your brain. It's just a matter of revealing that information to yourself."

I was deep in thought about Sal's words as the guard led me back to my cell. So much so that I don't think I even heard the catcalls and rude statements on any conscious level. I had a feeling Sal was right. While he'd always been a little mystical about dreams and other superstitious things I scoffed at, I believed he was onto something. They say that we only use a small percentage of our brain's capacity, right? I also believed that sometimes the answer to our questions was already floating around somewhere in our heads.

True warriors have access to universal knowledge. Everything that is known, will be known, or has been known, is the warriors for the taking if only he knows how to open himself up to that plane of existence.

I spent the rest of the day in my cell in a near meditative state, turning over every piece of information I knew that could be connected to the murders, over and over again.

The next day I spent three hours in a jammed holding cell at the courthouse. I'd woken up at peace, but with no clear answer as to who the killer was. The first step was getting out of this hell hole.

While I waited, I cast sideways glances at the two other inmates in my holding cell. We were all waiting for a guard to come get us and take us into the nearby courtroom. The two black women had amazing hair. One had a sleek red bob. The other had a close-cropped cut that framed her heart-shaped face perfectly.

Me? My Italian hair could not be tamed. I was pretty sure I looked homeless and would not make a good impression on the judge who was going to consider granting my bail. I surreptitiously put some spit on my fingers and tried to smooth it down, but the woman with the shorn head sneered and said, "That's nasty. Now your hair smell like your nasty breath and still don't look good."

"Thanks." I rolled my eyes, but shrunk further into my little corner of the bench.

The women talked about some dude named Jamal and how they were going to "kick his scrawny little ass" for letting them get arrested and how the Salinas jails were so much nicer than the San Jose ones.

"I ain't hooking in Gilroy no more," said the short-haired one with the heart-shaped face and small pink lips. "That place is a garlic reeking cesspool. I smell like garlic for like two days afterward."

It was the woman who said my breath was nasty.

Finally, a guard took her away.

The other girl gave me a sideways glance.

"Don't worry, mama, we all got bad breath in the can. You get used to it."

I looked at her for the first time and gave a small smile. I self-consciously smoothed my hair again.

"Champagne, she just a freak about hygiene, you know. Every time she locked up, she spends all her money on mints and gum and toothpaste and deodorant," the woman smiled and shrugged. "We all got our things, you know."

"Amen," I said, shaking my head. If being a hygiene freak was Champagne's only character defect, she was doing pretty good.

I got in front of the judge, gave Sal a glance, and in a flash, it was over. I wasn't sure what happened. When the gavel slammed down, I realized I was free. For now. But I had to stay in town.

CHAPTER THIRTY-SIX

SAL DROVE ME TO MY parents' house in his Aston Martin. I felt guilty sitting on his pristine leather seats in my filthy clothes. I didn't want to talk because I remembered Champagne's comment and didn't want him to smell my breath in the small interior. At first, he didn't say anything either and I thought about resting my head back and taking a quick nap.

Before I could fall asleep, Sal threw an envelope in my lap. I peeked inside. Hundred dollar bills. A fat stack of them.

"Ten grand."

He explained that now that he knew where I was, he could start fronting me money from my parents' trust until my godfather's estate was settled. But there was more.

"Want to know the good news or bad news first?"

"Good," I said with a sigh, looking out over the hills for a glimpse of the Monterey Bay.

"The good news is you are going to be one of the richest young ladies in northern California. Along with your inheritance from your parent's, you have everything Vito owned. He left everything to you. I'm still looking into it, but that appears to be a substantial amount of money. The bad news is this gives you more than enough motive in a jury's eyes to have killed Vito."

"Fuck."

"By the way," Sal said. "Did you know your saintly mother never said a swear word in her entire life?"

"Yes, Sal. She also never played pool or drank beer. She was freaking Princess Diana before Diana was a princess."

Sal chuckled and made the sign of the cross.

"Maybe you inherited some of that, I don't know. What I do know is that we got lucky today." He kept his eyes on the curving road in front of him. I kept my eyes on the giant sand dunes to our right. "Judge Aronsen and I — well, let's just say we know each other. You're damn lucky he was assigned your case. I talked to him in chambers beforehand and he told me if you skipped bail, he could cut off my balls. Now, I like my balls. I would be very upset if they had to go. You'll stay at your parents' house until the trial. *Capisco?* So, I can keep my balls. Keep the doors locked. Don't answer them for nobody. I got two guys coming over tonight and they'll be your security detail. They'll keep you out of trouble and make sure trouble don't come visit you."

"I get it, Sal. I'm not going anywhere."

He gave me the side-eye.

I returned his look with a huge smile.

CHAPTER THIRTY-SEVEN

OF COURSE, I LIED.

I was going back up to the city as fast as I could and before Sal's goons came over to keep me prisoner.

When Sal's Aston Martin slipped back down my parents' driveway, I quickly showered, brushed my teeth and grabbed some slacks and a sweater from my mother's closet. The panel had been returned and all my mother's clothing had been hung back up by the maid. I didn't stick around to get sentimental. I rummaged in a drawer in the kitchen and found a giant ring of keys to the four cars in the garage — A convertible Mercedes, a Range Rover, a Lincoln town car, and a Karmann Ghia my mother liked to drive. I chose the Range Rover. It had tinted and bullet proof glass. I needed to be in a vehicle that said I wasn't fucking around.

I'd taped a note for the goons on my bedroom door telling them I had taken a sleeping pill. I locked the bedroom door from within and climbed out the window. It might fool them until morning. If I was lucky. And I usually wasn't.

I PULLED INTO MY TENDERLOIN neighborhood at a little after five. The street was deserted. And my building looked like a squat. Windows and doors were boarded and police tape stretched across the entryway.

I racked my brains trying to figure out where could I find Thanh-Thanh. I had no idea. I parked in front of Café Katrina and headed inside.

I ordered a tequila. That eerily beautiful Asian bartender filled my glass without question every time I downed it. God, I loved this neighborhood.

I wanted to go on the wagon. And I'd made it for a while when I first moved into the Tenderloin. But now I had no reason to stay sober. I'd lost everyone in my family. I had no idea why. Someone wanted me dead, too. And I was probably going to spend the rest of my life in prison for a murder I didn't commit. Fuck everything. I didn't know how to dig myself out of any of it. But I did know lots about getting shitfaced.

I pushed my empty glass toward the bartender again and gave her my most winning, if drunken, smile. She gave me a stony look, but refilled the glass.

I'd never heard the bartender speak one single word. She never smiled, either. She'd just nod in response to everything anyone said. She always seemed extremely bored, too. Didn't she know she could get a job anywhere? After my fifth glass of tequila, I decided it was high time I told her this.

"You know," I said, dimly noting that my voice was slurred. "You could do much better than these digs. I know places on Union Street where you'd attract like, I don't know, maybe like five hundred guys a night who would drink there just to look at you — I mean that in the best way."

She gave me a look.

"No, it's not just the booze talking here. I mean it. These guys are loaded, filthy fuck rich and they would tip you, I don't know like, a hundred bucks a drink, just to get you to smile."

She rolled her eyes at that.

People around me at the bar started murmuring in agreement and I took that as encouragement to go on.

"No, really," I went on with my slurred words and all. Now everyone at the bar was paying attention. "Do you ever even look in the mirror? Why do you work in this dump, anyway?"

Everyone sitting at the bar around me grew silent.

The bartender's eyes narrowed and she drew her shoulders back. Then, she stuck out her hand. "Maybe it's time I introduce myself," she said in a brilliantly British accent. "I'm Katrina. The owner of this dump."

"Oh, fuck me." I put my head on the bar, ashamed, as the other people in the bar burst into laughter. I lifted my head. "I'm such an ass. I'm so sorry. Is there anything I can say to make it up to you?"

She stared at me for a second. Then reached over and refilled my glass.

It wasn't until two hours later when it was just me, Katrina, and some couple making out in the corner, that she spoke again.

"You're right. This is a dump," she said. "Right now. But it's my dump. I cashed out my retirement savings to buy it. I own the whole building. I'm working on getting investors to fix it up. I've got big plans. I'm going to renovate the bar, put in a kitchen in the back and serve comfort food, pot roast, mashed potatoes, you know the stuff all us San Francisco transplants crave. I'm going to gut the old industrial spaces above and make loft apartments for artists. I believe in the Tenderloin and I'm going to invest in it."

She met my eyes. She was dead serious. And determined.

I stared back and then gave a slow smile, raising my glass to her.

In my dim, foggy, alcohol-sodden brain, I wondered how much she'd need to make her dream come true.

CHAPTER THIRTY-EIGHT

I WOKE TO A SNEAKER prodding my stomach.

I groaned.

"Good. You alive. You look dead. What the fuck you doing on sidewalk like homeless lady? I come to check for trespassers and what I find? You. My tenant. Sleeping in gutter! Jesuuuuus!"

Trang.

I pried open my sleep-crusted eyes. Bad idea. Letting in the daylight made my head hurt even worse.

"What time is it?" I mumbled.

"Time for you to get your ass off sidewalk."

He grabbed me under the armpits and hoisted me to my feet. I still hadn't opened my eyes. I groaned.

"Is there anything left in my place?"

He shook his head no. "It all cleared out now. Thanh-Thanh got some of your stuff. Not much, I think," he paused for a second. "Gia, why you here? You have no place to sleep now?"

I opened my eyes. He looked concerned.

"Everyone else at Red Cross shelter. I take you there," he said.

"Thanks. But I need to find Django and Thanh-Thanh."

"They at the church. For now. Nobody knows where to go after that. I have insurance on building, but it's not enough."

"You're the owner?" I was shocked. I'd thought he was the building manager.

He looked slightly embarrassed.

"Yes. I'm owner. I don't want my tenants to know. They think I too big for my britches, you know? I don't want them to feel intimidated. All tenants – except you — old ladies my mom was friends with. I want them to think they are taking care of themselves and no burden to me. I only charge them two hundred dollar for their apartments. They think that is normal rent for people. My way of paying back my mother. She died, but she wanted me to take care of her friends so they don't end up on streets. Now, I don't know what to do. They too old to work. They can't pay regular rent, prices too high, you know."

I blinked twice and drew back to look at Trang.

"Jesus Fucking Christ. You're a saint. A god damn saint. Right under the same roof as me and I didn't even know. Trang," I looped my arm through his. "I got a plan. I got money and I got a plan. Don't you worry another second about where you and your mother's little old lady friends are going to live. I got it all taken care of. On one condition, though?"

He narrowed his eyes at me. "What?"

"If I don't go to prison for murder — and that's a big 'if' — you let me and Django live in the same building as you guys again. I'll take care of getting the building — it will still be in this neighborhood. Maybe we'll raze the building and rebuild right here. But I want to live there, too with all of you. That's my offer."

I stuck out my hand.

He chewed his lip for a minute, eyeing my outstretched fingers. I waited. I stopped myself from rolling my eyes. Like there was anything to think about.

"Deal," he shook my hand.

I needed to see Thanh-Thanh and Django. But first I had a stop to make.

CHAPTER THIRTY-NINE

WHEN I WALKED OUT OF the police station, I slumped against the brick wall and waited for my heart to stop racing.

Ethel had been strangled. And they had found something stuffed down her throat. A playing card. The detective asked me if the one-eyed jack had any significance to me.

That's when I knew. Her murder was a warning. For me.

The warrior knows that despite physical strength and training, if one's strength is solely physical and not interwoven with the spirit, then achieving a true state of Budo is impossible. Physical and spiritual strength must be equal. A peaceful heart is necessary to achieve full strength. A desire to protect the innocent is the foundation of all a warrior's actions.

Outside the station, my eyes began to sting. "I'll get them for this Ethel." I started to say I was sorry when I felt a tear slip out the corner of my eye. I angrily swatted it away. I looked around at the people who were walking by and eyeballing me. I didn't have time to cry.

Suddenly, I was filled with fear. I couldn't get to the church fast enough and relief filled me when I saw Thanh-Thanh's smiling face.

A dozen cots had been set up in the basement of Saint Boniface church. All the rest of the little old Vietnamese ladies sat at a table playing cards. Django looked up briefly and wagged his tail when I walked in, but clearly Thanh-Thanh had replaced me as master. Fine by me. She was more responsible than I was anyway.

"They let you keep dogs here?"

Thanh-Thanh didn't answer. But she was beaming. She leaned over and rummaged in a bag and came out with my mother's box.

Miracles of miracles. My mother's box had survived the fire. It smelled like smoke, but it was intact.

Her smile lit up her face. I held my hand to my heart and pressed my lips together tightly to hold back the emotions swarming through me. I took the box, hugged her wordlessly, and then turned on my heel to leave.

"Gia? Okay?" she called to my back.

I nodded and put up my hand behind me to wave goodbye. I didn't trust myself to talk. I'd be back later.

Sitting in the Range Rover, I flipped through my dad's love letters, holding some of them up to my nose to see if they smelled like my mother. They didn't. I held them to my chest. I felt something small and hard. In the middle of all the love letters was a blank envelope. With something inside.

I dumped it out. A key on a small gold chain.

A tiny tag attached to the key had writing in my mother's flowy handwriting.

It said, "#25, City of the Dead."

A memory came zooming back.

When Christopher and I were very little, around five, our father left on a long business trip. The day after he left, our mother had told us she was taking us on a field trip—a secret adventure to the City of the Dead.

Christopher and I giggled with both fear and excitement, knowing that our mother would never take us anywhere truly frightening, only someplace fun. On the drive up from Monterey, when Christopher tried to ask about our field trip, she'd put her finger up to her mouth and gestured to the driver. Then she said something loudly about all the shopping we were going to do at Sak's Fifth Avenue that day. She gave us large, exaggerated winks as she said this and we giggled, thrilled to be part of something secretive.

Our driver dropped us off at Union Square and my mother said something to him about picking us up later that day at the same spot, but instead of heading into Saks Fifth Avenue, my mom looked around and then grabbed us, making us run until we got to a stairway that led to the BART train tracks.

"This is going to be so much fun!" she said, but her voice was wavering. "We're going to ride a train."

"Yes!" Christopher shouted, pumping his fist into the air. But the tremble in my mother's voice scared me, so I clung to her side, for some reason struck with fear that she was going to run away and leave us on this underground train platform.

Instead, we got onto the train.

"When do we get off?" Christopher asked.

"Not until the very end of the line. The City of the Dead."

People got on the train and gave my mother looks. She was a stunningly beautiful woman and I didn't like the way the men looked at her. I clung to her arm and glared at the men in their smelly work clothes or their too big pants and big sneakers and headphones.

Slowly people got off at their stops until it was just the three of us and one sad looking elderly lady with a push cart full of groceries.

The announcer said something I couldn't understand as we pulled into the bright sunlight from beneath the earth.

"Here we are, my pets. Let's go visit the City of the Dead." My mother sounded like she was nervous but trying to sound cheerful, as if this were an adventure.

We blinked as we came off the train into the bright sunlight. She held tightly to both our hands. As we hurried along, the large purse she had on her shoulder kept swinging and bumping my face. My usually calm mother was snappish and had a tense look on her face.

"I just have one stop first." I stopped and looked up at her. A large crease had formed between her brows. It frightened me. My mother was usually cheerful and always smiling. I rarely saw her frown.

She led us into a small lobby of a post office. My eyes grew wide as she pulled a chain around her neck out from under her shirt. A tiny gold key was on the end of the chain. Her hands were slightly shaking as she stuck the key into a hole on a small box. She dug into her bag and was yanking out a stack of papers. She seemed flustered and some fell onto the ground. When I bent to get them for her, she pushed me away so I toppled over. When she realized what she had done, she clutched me to her chest and started crying.

It scared me so bad that I started crying, too. I pulled away. "Mama, it's okay. Please don't cry. I'm not even hurt."

"Shhhhhh," she said, breathing into my hair and then pulling back, kissing my face. "I'm sorry my love. I'm sorry."

Christopher didn't like the attention and pretended to slam his foot in the door, which caught my mother's attention. She stood, brushing herself off.

"Christopher, *stai zitto e basta*. I'm almost done here."

She shoved the papers inside the box and slammed it shut. For a few seconds, she closed her eyes and held her palm against the outside of the box. Her lips were murmuring as if she were saying a prayer.

Then, as if nothing had happened, she turned to us, brightly with a large smile.

"Let's go. I can't wait to see the City of the Dead."

But I was still confused and worried about how she'd been acting. "Did you mail something?" I asked.

"Something like that, sweetie. It's just a little errand."

By now, she'd led us outside. I looked around. It looked like anywhere else.

"Why do they call it the City of the Dead?"

Just then we passed a small plaque that said, "It's great to be alive in Colma."

"Well, there are more dead people here than alive people," my mother said. Now, for the first time all day, she seemed relaxed and back to her normal self.

"Yuck," I said and scowled. "Why did you want to show us this?"

Christopher punched me in the arm.

"Shut up, Gia. You big baby." He hugged my mom. "This is awesome, mama. I love it. Let's go look at the dead people."

My mother, who would always and forever break my heart, didn't scold Christopher for hitting me, but laughed with delight. "Oh, sweetheart, there aren't any dead people to see. Just gravestones."

As we walked, headed for a giant cemetery on the hill, my mother told us that in the old days people were not allowed to bury the dead within the San Francisco city limits, so they made this town on the outskirts, a burial spot.

"The town was founded as a necropolis in 1924," my mother said.

"What's a whatchamacallit?" I asked.

"A necropolis is basically a cemetery. In ancient times, large swaths of land outside cities were set aside to bury the dead. But think about this, this entire town of Colma was made just to be a cemetery. They say that more than two million bodies are buried here," she said, pointing to a population sign. "And look, only 1,200 people—who are alive—live here."

My mom blabbed on and on. I tried not to listen, but now, nearly twenty years later, I remembered everything she told us that day. She told us that Colma, which was only two square miles large, had seventeen cemeteries within its boundaries.

But at the time, I thought it was all useless information I didn't care about. She'd made such a big deal about this City of the Dead that I was supremely disappointed to find out it just meant a giant cemetery. Boring.

We wandered through Jewish, Chinese, Catholic cemeteries, modest ones with small plaques in the ground and elaborate ones with angel and Virgin Mary statues. There was even a pet cemetery.

We spent two hours walking up and down the rolling green hills, looking for the graves of famous people my mother had read were buried in Colma. We spotted the gravestones for Levi Strauss and William Randolph Hearst, but never could find Wyatt Earp or Joe DiMaggio's graves.

Later, after much grumbling on my part, we headed back to Union Square where my mother bought us lunch at the Cheesecake Factory, so I didn't consider the entire trip a waste. When my father came home, she told him about our field trip and we were required to regurgitate what we had learned. Christopher did most of the talking. I didn't say much. I was still thinking about how odd she had acted when she unlocked that little box and stuffed it with papers.

CHAPTER FORTY

WHATEVER MY MOTHER had put into that post office box years ago had something to do with all of this. Why else would she hide this key in her special papers? Like it was just yesterday, I remembered my mother's distress on our visit to the City of the Dead.

I looped the chain with the key around my neck, grabbed my jacket, and headed for the BART station on Market Street.

The train had almost reached the Colma station when I realized I'd been followed from my parking spot in front of the church.

Two men watched me through the doors dividing my train compartment from the next. One was on a cell phone.

I counted to ten and made a mad dash through the train door in front of me. I ran past startled passengers as fast as I could without bothering to see if the men were following. I made it all the way to the front of the train, near the driver's compartment, before I stopped to catch my breath. My arms were sore from shoving open the train doors between compartments. I looked behind me, but didn't see the two men. That didn't comfort me. I was sure they were back there somewhere. My plan was to jump off the train when it stopped and hide.

Once I was sure I had ditched them, I'd sneak into the post office and then back onto a train before they knew where I'd gone. I didn't take my eyes off the door connecting my train compartment with the one behind me, but didn't see any movement. I tried to glance through the glass doors all the way back, but as the train wove on the windy tracks, I could not see very far back. Then, the train burst topside and the night outside, lit with streetlights, was visible.

The driver of the train must have thought he was a comedian and was feeling chatty because as soon as the train pulled to a loud, screeching stop at the Colma station, he got on the crackling announcement system.

"Okay, folks. This is the end of the line. The Colma stop. The last stop on BART and the next to the last stop of the night. And frankly, the last stop for thousands of other people. But you don't need to worry about them. They're all underground. I'm out of here, but there is one more train stopping at this station tonight. It will leave here at midnight. That's forty-five minutes from now. So, if you don't plan on staying the night in the City of the Dead, I suggest you be back here in time to catch the midnight train."

Forty-five minutes. That meant I had to run as fast as I could. Not only to ditch the men following me, but to get the last train back to the city.

I glanced behind me as I stepped out the train doors. How fitting that the people who wanted me dead would find me here. At the end of the line. In the City of the Dead.

CHAPTER FORTY-ONE

I PUSHED THROUGH THE rush of people going through the turn style and ducked into a bathroom. I closed the door of the first stall and crouched on the seat, holding my knees to my chest so my feet were off the floor. I did a slow count to one hundred until the last echo of passing footsteps slowed. Then to be safe, I counted to one hundred again before I put my feet on the grimy bathroom floor and crept toward the door.

Before I opened it, I held my ear to the door to see if I could hear any noises outside. Then, I cracked the door an inch and peered out. The platform was empty. I inched it open even more and then drew back with a gasp when another eye met mine. It was a cleaning lady.

She held her hand to her heart and mumbled something in Spanish. I did a little bow of apology and slipped around her cleaning cart. There was not a body in sight in any direction.

To be safe, I walked the length of the platform and exited at a door that was at the opposite end of where the train had pulled in. I poked my head out into the night and didn't see anyone at all on the streets, which were lit with pockets of orange that glowed in the fog. I was grateful for the fog.

After I got my bearings, I headed for the post office. I crouched in the doorway of the business next door, waiting to see if I'd been followed. The streets were deserted. I crept over to the post office and was grateful that the interior lights didn't flicker on when I entered the lobby. It only took me a moment to find #25. Again, I looked around and looked for movement outside the big glass storefront windows, but didn't see a soul. I fished for the necklace and drew it out of my shirt. The key fit. I stuck my hand inside and closed my eyes, for some reason afraid of what I would find. My hand closed around a small bundle of envelopes. Letters? I glanced down. These were addressed to my mother in a different handwriting than the ones exchanged between my mother and father.

With Italian postage.

I shoved them into the inside pocket of my coat and then reached into the box to see if there was anything else. My hand felt only cold metal.

I closed the box, leaving the key inside the lock. I had no use for it anymore.

I glanced at my phone. Thirty-five minutes until the last train back to San Francisco. I needed to be back in Monterey before Sal found out I was gone.

With my thoughts so much on the letters, I wasn't as careful as I should've been and stepped onto the sidewalk without looking out the storefront window first. I'm not sure I would've spotted them, but at least I might've had a chance.

Two men at the far end of the block emerged from the fog. I could see their arms raise as they saw me. I looked frantically around. The only place to run was into the graveyard to my left. I didn't hesitate.

In the silence of the night, I could hear heavy breathing and footsteps pounding behind me as I raced through the gated entryway to the graveyard. At first I ran in a straight line and then decided I better zig zag and head toward a corner to hide. The cemetery was on a hill a little bit above downtown Colma, so the fog wasn't as thick. The night was lit up by an orange glow of city lights reflecting on a low layer of clouds above. Just light enough for me to see where I was going, but not enough light for anyone to see very far. I raced, heart pounding until I came across a stretch of giant structures, mausoleums and elaborate statues to honor the dead.

The graveyard was massive — the biggest one in Colma. These guys could look all night and maybe not find me. At least that's what I was hoping. I scooted up against the wall of one of the mausoleums, on the far side facing the big wrought iron fence that surrounded the cemetery. It took me a bit to catch my breath. I listened but didn't hear any sound. How smart were these men? I had a feeling they knew what the hell they were doing. That meant one guy was probably hanging out near the entrance to the cemetery while the other one looked for me. I eyed the iron fence. I didn't think I could scale it. I also couldn't fit between the bars. I was trapped in a cemetery, being hunted by two goons.

I had to think of a plan. Not for the first time tonight, I wished I had my gun. It was somewhere in a police evidence locker.

Then, I heard the snap of a twig and all my senses electrified. Someone was near.

I scooted into a little alcove formed by the doorway of the mausoleum and tried to press myself as tightly as I could against it. It moved a little. I froze. Was there a chance the door was unlocked? Even so, it probably would make a god-awful screeching or creaking noise if I opened the door. The sound of footsteps on dried leaves grew closer. He was heading my way. I didn't have a choice. If the door opened I needed to hide inside. If the noise alerted him to my whereabouts, I'd try to lock the door from the inside. Or I'd be trapped. It was hard to say. I'd have to take my chances.

I reached up and turned the knob while I pressed my back against the door. It silently opened. I scrambled inside and shut the door behind me. Slits high up on the ceiling let in enough light for me to see there weren't any windows. I rummaged around in my bag and found a lighter. I snapped it on and saw that I could lock the door from the inside. I slid the lock closed and looked at my phone. I had twenty-five minutes to catch the last train out of Colma unless I intended to stay the night in the cemetery — not something I was interested in doing.

I'd wait here for five minutes, until the men outside had moved on, and then make a run for the gate.

I put the flashlight app on my phone and peered around the mausoleum. It was just as creepy as I'd imagined. A coffin was in the center of the room.

The stack of letters crumpled uncomfortably in my inside pocket. I extracted the stack and with shaking hands unfolded the first letter. What was so important my mom had to hide these? Who was she hiding them from? And why?

The first letter was in Italian.

It was a love letter. From Turricci. I gasped as I read it.

My unfamiliarity with some Italian and his flowing script made it hard at first to decipher what he was saying. He was apologizing for something. When I figured it out, I felt sick. He was my mother's guardian and yet he was in love with her and forced himself on her? She had to flee Italy to America. He wrote that he was saddened that she hated him so much and hoped she would one day forgive him. He begged her to leave my father. Turricci said he tried to make up for his "past indiscretions" by buying her land and a villa. He said he would never give up as long as he lived. There was much more. I skimmed the four pages and then put it in my outside coat pocket. I picked up the next envelope.

This one was filled with vitriol. It practically jumped off the page. In it, Turricci accused my mother of ruining his life. He said he was unable to love anyone else and that he would rather see her dead than see her with my father. He included a clipping of my father and mother that had run in the Monterey Herald newspaper. They were at a fundraiser at Pebble Beach golf course. I traced my mother's face in the faded newspaper picture. She was looking up at my father adoringly.

My father's face was scratched out with pen. The pen had ripped a hole where my father's face had been.

My heart was pounding. There was more. The letters spanned twenty-three years. The last letter was dated shortly before my mother's death. In it, Turricci said that he would not rest until she was dead. Any love he'd ever felt for her had evaporated. He would never forgive her for taking his child away, he wrote.

I couldn't get air into my lungs. My face felt like ice. My vision grew fuzzy. This was the proof I had been looking for, but it came bundled with a jagged knife that ripped open the fabric of my world, exposing a reality I had never imagined in my worst nightmares.

He was my father.

With hands shaking madly, I quickly flipped through the letter to the last page, printed on different paper. It was my birth certificate.

I smoothed out the creases and tried to focus on the name after the word: father. Mateo Antonio Turricci was my father.

My stomach heaved. I shoved all the papers in my pocket and lunged for the door. I didn't care if the men were outside waiting for me, I needed air. I needed to run.

I yanked open the door and ran, gasping and crying as I headed toward the front gate of the cemetery, not caring who saw me. I had fifteen minutes to make it to the train. They wouldn't dare kill me on the train with all its cameras. I had a head start and I would make it. I knew it.

CHAPTER FORTY-TWO

THE ENTRANCE TO THE gate was twenty feet in front of me by the time I heard panting and footsteps crunching behind me. I knew if they had guns, I was within shooting distance. I could hear them talking to one another.

"There! To your right."

I turned and came at the iron fence at a running start and used a nearby headstone as a stepping stone that propelled me halfway up the fence. I clutched the metal bars and shimmied my way up. By this time, the men were at the bottom. I expected my leg to be yanked and to fall to the ground, but miraculously, I was inches from their reach. I half-expected the roar of a gunshot as I flung my leg over the pointed barb at the top. My coat caught as I tried to swing my other leg over and came down on another spear-like barb. The pain took my breath away and made me lose my grip completely. I would've fallen to the ground except a big fat chunk of my thigh was impaled on this barb.

The voices below me grew dim and I concentrated on not passing out as I gripped the fence as tight as I could and lifted my leg, slowly off the barb, hoping that I wouldn't bleed to death from taking it out. Gingerly, I felt where the hole was. Instead of a gushing foundation of blood from my artery, I only felt some dampness spreading. I would live. For now.

I slipped to the other side and pushed myself away from the fence so the men's greedy hands wouldn't grab me as I fell. I landed in a ball and cried out in pain from the pressure of landing on my injured leg.

I didn't wait to see what the men had planned, but they clearly couldn't scale the fence. As I race-walked and limped away I heard this:

"Mr. Turricci, *per la stazione ferroviaria.*"

Good God. He was here. And he was after me. He was the one who wanted me dead. My own father. The name listed as my father on my birth certificate.

I kept running, breathing loudly as I hobbled through the fog. I saw the sign for the train. I was almost there. I dipped into the entrance to BART, limping painfully and hoping it wasn't too late.

The platform was deserted and a few lights were out, making it even dimmer than normal. I headed for the far end of the platform and ducked into the shadows behind a pillar close to the tracks. My blood raced and I could hear the pounding of my heart in my ears. My body shook as I silently prayed for the train to come. I clutched the incriminating documents inside my coat, wadding them up into a tight ball in the palm of my sweaty hand. My legs shook uncontrollably and I reached down to see if more blood had come out.

I heard the distant rumble down the tracks. The train was almost here. Far, far down the tunnel, I could see the smallest glow from the headlights of the BART train. Only a few more seconds. I could still make it. If the train came right now, I could slip inside and maybe it would pull away before he caught up to me. But then I heard it, the sound of someone running.

The pounding of footsteps grew closer. I heard someone shout my name. Someone with a thick Italian accent. A voice that was disturbingly familiar, as if my very cells recognized him at my core. Giving one last glance down the tracks at the oncoming train, I knew it was too late. I was out of time.

I turned to face this man. I was going to get my very first glimpse of my own father: the man who raped and murdered my mother. A dark figure in a trench coat hurtled down the stairs, hopped the turn style and then ran into the light.

As train roared into the station, filling the tunnel with light and sound, the man's face was illuminated. I gasped, the air sucked out of my lungs.

Mateo Antonio Turricci was the man I'd tried so desperately to sleep with at the hotel in Sicily. My vision started to close in and my legs gave out. I felt myself slumping, falling off the platform and onto the tracks.

CHAPTER FORTY-THREE

I WOKE CONFUSED. THE last thing I remember was being yanked from the edge of the tracks. I was in a big bed. I pulled myself up onto my elbows and glanced around with blurry eyes.

The room was glowing orange, lit by a dying blaze in a giant fireplace I could stand up in. The room contained velvet upholstered chairs, gorgeous oil paintings, and a goon asleep on a folding chair in the corner. He was snoring.

Then I noticed my clothes were on a chair beside the bed. I glanced down. I was wearing a silky nightgown.

It all came back to me and I was horrified. I'd tried to sleep with my own father. No wonder he had reacted so violently when I kissed him. I felt sick. Not only was he my father, but he was also the person who raped and killed my mother. I leaned over and dry heaved over the side of the bed. I had nothing left in me.

I clutched for my clothes and drew them to my chest. My jacket crackled. The letters were still inside.

Reaching into my jacket pocket and keeping my eye on the man in the corner, I painstakingly withdrew the letters, slowly, slowly so they didn't make any noise. There was still one envelope I hadn't opened. I looked at it carefully. It had never been opened. The postal mark was after my mother's death.

Heart pounding, without taking my eyes off the gorilla in the corner, I quietly slit open the envelope with a fingernail. It was from a

DNA service. It had my name on it. My mother must have snuck something from me to garner my DNA.

I knew it was a fairly new capacity – to be able to check someone's DNA instead of doing a paternity test. I wondered why she had never done a paternity test with my father. Then I realized. My father—the man who raised me and the man I loved more than any other man in the world—hadn't known. He'd always assumed I was his daughter.

My heart broke for her right then. What a horrid secret to keep.

With shaking fingers, I read on.

It had my father's name on it: Lorenzo Santella. 99 percent likelihood.

I sagged with relief and tears spurted out of my eyes. Turricci was not my father.

But the letter had been dated after my mother's death. She had never known. She had died before learning I wasn't Turricci's daughter.

As my heart rate slowed, all the puzzle pieces clicked into place. It all made sense, now. My entire life made sense.

No wonder my mother loved Christopher. He was her love child with my father – or the man I believed was my father. The love of her life.

Me? My whole life my mother had believed that I was the product of a rape. A rape by this man, Turricci. A killer. A monster. A man my mother loathed. When she looked at me, she must have seen the man she hated. But she still loved me. I knew she loved me. Not as much as she loved, Christopher, though.

If she had lived, she would've known I wasn't Turricci's daughter. But she would never know now. This man, Turricci, had cheated me out of the true love my mother should have had for me. Hatred surged through me. I crumpled the papers loudly in my fist.

The man across the room startled awake and I quickly shoved the papers back in my jacket pocket.

He acknowledged me with a grunt and then leaned over and knocked on the door.

A few minutes later, Turricci walked in. He met my eyes and nodded.

"You know now, don't you?"

I didn't answer.

"I wanted so much to tell you in Sicily, but you left. I wanted to explain why I couldn't make love to you. Why my love for you is infinitely deeper than a love a man has for a woman."

He leaned down and kissed my brow. I struggled to get away from him and tried to spit in his face, but it only came straight back down and dribbled down my chin.

He patiently took out a silk handkerchief and gently wiped my face. I started swinging and connected once with his jaw before I was pushed back into the pillow from a hand that came out of nowhere.

The gorilla was holding me down. Turricci didn't react.

"When you walked into my hotel, I knew who you were immediately. I've kept tabs on you since I found out that you were mine."

I glared.

"Your brother was the one who contacted me. He let me know that you were my daughter."

"What?" I had vowed not to talk, but this news startled me.

"He found your birth certificate. He sent me a copy."

Anger flared through me.

"Is that why you killed Christopher?"

"No. I didn't kill your brother. Only your mother."

His words sent me thrashing toward him, wind milling my arms at him, teeth bared, fingernails at the ready, swearing at him, ready to tear his throat open. But the goon flattened me back on the pillow with one beefy arm. A screaming pain shot up from my leg like an electrical jolt and had me gasping. I realized then how hurt I was. I glanced down and saw a thick bandage around my thigh. Someone had given me medical care, but the pain was still intense.

I closed my eyes.

This man before me killed my mother and father. I would not rest until I had avenged them. I needed to make a plan. I needed to escape so I could kill this man before me.

But Turricci was not done talking.

"When your mother left me brokenhearted in Sicily, I thought my life was over. I believed that without her love I was doomed to be alone. So, I plotted. I made plans to win her back. I wrote her and begged her and offered her, not only my heart, but all my earthly belongings."

He closed his eyes for a second.

"But she didn't want me."

Slowly, my love for her grew into hate. I had never hated anything or anyone as desperately as I hated your mother. I hated your father, too. But he was just a pawn. It was your mother who ruined my life.

I prayed every day that my hatred would lessen.

I thought I had accepted your mother's betrayal. But then I made the mistake of going to Geneva during the fete season and saw your parents.

They were dancing in a corner at the gala and when I saw the way your mother looked at your father I knew that my hatred would never dissipate until your mother was dead.

He paused and I stared at him. "Why did you try to cover it up?"

"I didn't. Not at first. The fire was an unfortunate result of my cigarette. But then I got the letter from Christopher. It came the next day, before he knew about the fire. It was then that I knew I had to cover up the murders. I knew that I needed to make sure suspicion never fell on me because if it did you would never accept me as your father."

I narrowed my eyes at him. My fists clenched at my sides. If I had a knife I would leap out of bed and stab him right in the jugular.

He had killed everyone I cared about.

"Why did you kill Ethel?"

He tilted his head and frowned.

"The homeless lady? The one who lived outside my building in the Tenderloin. You know the one you burned down?"

He shook his head. "My men started the fire, yes, but I don't know this Ethel you speak of."

Liar. I scowled.

"Why did you kill Vito?"

He sighed and nodded. "Yes, the old man's blood is on my hands. But it is entirely his fault. He didn't need to get involved. You see, he had complicated things. Vito, your mother's precious friend, had run your father's company into the ground with his gambling debts. It was not my problem. Until he suspected I was behind the murders. Then he tried to blackmail me. He wanted me to pay an exorbitant sum for a mediocre development in San Francisco. He was a fool. He'd been gone from the old country so long that he'd forgotten who he was dealing with. He was so Americanized. He had grown soft. You don't blackmail Mateo Turricci. What a fool."

"He was a good man." I said, glowering.

Turricci shrugged. "He wasn't as foolish as I thought. He'd actually drawn up a will leaving everything to you right before he died. I think he wanted the money so you would be provided for since he had squandered your inheritance. I think he may have been trying to put things right."

I swallowed the lump that had risen to my throat, remembering the look in Vito's eyes as I pressed a blade against his fleshy neck. He died thinking I hated him.

Because of this fucker.

"I hate you." I spit the words out.

Turricci sighed.

"You do now. But that will change. You are my flesh and blood and nothing can change that." His gaze was piercing.

Something could change that. A nice crisp piece of paper in my jacket. But I was biding my time. I'd eyed the fireplace poker and was calculating how quickly I could get to it and if I could beat the goon to get to Turricci.

"One of my greatest fears has been to die alone," he said. "I could have the most beautiful woman in the world as my wife, but I would always question whether she was with me for my money. But when you have *la famiglia*. When you have children. They are there for love and honor. *L'affetto verso i genitori e fondamento di ogni virtu.*"

I rolled my eyes. He was spouting Italian proverbs about children being there for their parents. He continued.

"Now, I've connected with my own flesh and blood, my own child. I will not die alone. *Il sangue non è acqua.*" Blood is thicker than water.

With those words, I knew I had one last card to play and that I better play it fast.

CHAPTER FORTY-FOUR

AS TURRICCI CONTINUED to mumble nonsense about our undeniable family likeness, I assessed my situation.

I was injured, vulnerable. I had no gun. I couldn't use my body, my Budo training, because of my injured leg. I'd trained for years to not be weak in situations like this. And yet, here I was. I needed to get to the fireplace poker. But I needed some advantage if I were going to be able to use it.

All I had left was my mind.

That's what Budo taught me. The melding of spiritual, physical, and mental strength.

In this case, my words, not my hands or legs, were my only weapons.

I would choose them carefully.

The truth was my only weapon.

Turricci kept talking, occasionally leaning over me with a confusing glimmer of kindness in his eyes.

"You will inherit everything I have. You are my only flesh and blood. I will take you home to the villa — now it is yours. You will love it. Everything I have is yours."

I pressed my lips tightly together and shook my head. At that moment despite myself, I felt pity for this unlovable man.

"No?" he seemed genuinely surprised. "Because I killed your mother? You will forgive me for that. It may take time, but I am a patient man. You are all I have left. You will learn to love me. She poisoned you against me."

I narrowed my eyes. "Your name never crossed her lips. You weren't important enough for her to talk about. She never said anything to me about you."

He didn't answer but the clench of his jaw said it all.

I waited a few seconds, trying not to look at the fireplace poker. I needed him to be upset. To lose his cool. I needed something crazy to happen if I were going to get to that poker.

"There is something you need to know."

He raised an eyebrow.

"There are some letters in my jacket you need to see."

I reached for my jacket, but the gorilla put out an arm and pressed me back into the bed. Turricci nodded and the gorilla reached inside the inner pocket of my jacket and took out the envelopes. He handed them to Turricci.

I held my breath watching as Turricci read his own love letters and then turned to the birth certificate. He took the paper and unfolded it with a smile.

"Look at the paper underneath."

He shuffled the papers and began to read. The smile faded and his face grew ashen. He looked up at me, stricken.

I grinned. "I'm not your daughter."

CHAPTER FORTY-FIVE

"LEAVE US ALONE."

His voice was broken, a shadow of the confident man he'd been seconds before. At first his henchman didn't move. Turricci said something in Italian and the man slowly got up, casting a malevolent glance my way, and walked out.

It could not have gone any better. I could take on Turricci alone even with a bum leg.

He paced the room. "It can't be true. That night, I know we made a child. I know it."

He was talking to himself.

"I don't want to die alone." He stopped at the window and drew back the curtain.

As soon as he turned his back I was out of the bed in one smooth motion with the poker in front of me. Wincing in pain, I swung the poker around to him.

"You killed my parents and Vito and now you have to die." My voice was steady. My hand steadier. I ignored the screaming pain shooting up my leg.

He turned and stared at me. "Have you ever killed somebody, Gia?"

His voice was calm. My heart sank. I was weak. He knew it. I swallowed back my fear.

He smiled. "You aren't a killer."

"You don't know that."

"I think I do."

"You have to die. You killed my parents. I have to avenge their death. You are from the old country. You know this. You know that I have no honor unless I kill you."

He shrugged. "Maybe the old ways are dying."

"That may be true. But I cannot live with myself knowing you are alive."

He closed his eyes and breathed in deeply before opening them again.

Then, he nodded.

For a second that felt like an eternity, we stared at one another.

"Freeze!" someone shouted.

Then, to my surprise, Turricci smiled and before I could comprehend it, he lunged for the poker, charging until it slid neatly into his chest. For another second, he was upright his eyes glimmering with something I didn't understand. And then the light left them and he slumped. We both fell to the ground. I let go shrieking and crying and trying to get away from his body.

Distantly I realized that Sal and two police officers with guns drawn stood in the doorway.

Sal was instantly at my side, propping me up and holding me close.

"You were supposed to stay in Monterey."

"I'm sorry," I said.

"You're free to go now. I just got off the phone with the judge. All charges against you have been dropped."

I looked at him in confusion and he continued. "We've got Turricci for the murders of your parents and your godfather."

"How'd you find me?"

"Wasn't really you we found. We've had eyes on Turricci. He owns this place. When he showed up here early this morning, we headed up from Monterey. We knew he was behind it the whole time. It was just a matter of proving it."

"Oh." I didn't know what else to say.

"Where do you want to go? You still own your place on Russian Hill. Want me to take you there?"

I nodded in a daze.

CHAPTER FORTY-SIX

I SPENT THE NEXT WEEK huddled in my old bed. Every once in a while, I took a sip of water or a small bite of cracker. Other than that, I kept a constant stream of sleeping pills in my body. I wished I could add a lethal dose of booze to the mix but someone had cleared out my apartment of all my hidden stashes of drugs and alcohol. I didn't have energy to do anything but lay in bed.

Most of the time I was awake I replayed Turricci's death over and over in my mind. Did he charge me because he wanted the police to shoot me? Or did he charge me because he knew I couldn't kill him myself? Or was it something else?

Sal stopped by and said that Vito had spent every last dime from my father's seafood company trying to repay gambling debts. I didn't care. But then he said I was far from destitute, Turricci had left his vast fortune to me."

I wasn't sure if I was having a mental break or was in a deep depression, but I didn't do a whole lot except get up to use the bathroom maybe once a day. Some lady Sal had hired let herself in once a day to set a bunch of finger foods by my bed and occasionally I'd take a bite or two, even though it all tasted like cardboard.

On the fourth day, Dante let himself in with my spare key.

I cried and told him everything as he held me in his arms.

Finally, when he had wiped all my tears and snot away he held my chin up with one finger and looked me in the eyes.

"Your mother loved you, Gia. I know that for sure."

"Dante, she died thinking I was the product of her rape."

"That didn't matter to her, did it?"

"I don't know."

I stared at the ceiling until he left.

The next day he came back.

This time he made me shower and eat some fried eggs, but I threw them up.

Later that day, I woke to find my bedroom filled with faces. Taking in my friends, Thanh-Thanh, Trang, Kato, Susie, their kids, Darling, even Django.

Dante and his mother stood in the corner with their arms around each other, beaming.

I took in all the faces before me and burst into tears.

I did have a family. I had people who loved me and that's what family really was. It wasn't the people I was tied to by blood. Despite being brainwashed my entire life by mother culture and family — my family was much more than those who shared my bloodline. My family was of my own making.

That realization gave me the strength to live.

CHAPTER FORTY-SEVEN

THREE MONTHS LATER …

Before the opening night party, I stopped by the Sunset View Cemetery in Berkeley carting two dozen red roses. I had made sure Ethel was buried in a spot high on a hill that overlooked the San Francisco Bay.

I spread the roses out on her grave and tried not to cry.

"I'm sorry you got such a bum break in this world, Ethel," I sniffed. "You didn't deserve it. That man, your husband, the creep you killed a long time ago. I'm glad you killed him. I should've told you that when you were alive. That I'm happy you killed him. I hope he's looking down seeing how I'm bringing you two dozen red roses instead of his cheap dozen he thought would convince you to put up with his crap. I made arrangements, Ethel. You're going to have a dozen roses delivered here every week. It's the least I can do. I should've been a better friend to you. I'm so god damn sorry. I'm so, so sorry. It's my curse. Everyone who knows me ends up dead. I'm so sorry we met. All I can do is tell you that you mattered. You mattered to me. And there are going to be roses on your grave for as long as I live. That way everyone who walks by this grave will know you were somebody who mattered. And you know, what? You're right. You were free. You lived your life the way you wanted and you were free."

I suddenly had something in my eye. I walked away, blinking.

When I walked into Café Katrina, my tears had dried and I'd fixed my makeup. I was excited to see the inside of the place. Katrina had been so secretive about it the past month.

When I walked in, I was astonished. It was gorgeous, with tall ceilings, giant silver and crystal chandeliers, plush purple velvet booths, blue velvet wallpaper, wall-sized silver framed mirrors and black marble floors.

"Unbelievable," I said when I saw Katrina. "You are a true artist. This is stunning."

"That's what I was going for," she said dryly.

Katrina led me over to a booth raised on a small platform. It has black velvet curtains on each side.

"This is your booth."

"What?"

"Look," she led me over to the plush purple velvet booth. There was a silver plaque just above the cushion that said, "Gia Santella."

"You're kidding?"

"Nope. Why don't you sit down and test it out? It has the best view in the place."

Again, I felt like something was in my eye. I gave her a kiss on the cheek and said, "Go greet your guests! This is your night. I'm going to sit here and relax while you be social. That's what a silent partner does. They don't have to talk."

She threw back her head and laughed.

Just then the mayor walked in. I was impressed until I saw the governor behind him. I watched Katrina greet them and lead them to another velvet booth. I saw the mayor nod approvingly at the governor as they followed her. A few minutes later, a famous Hollywood actor walked in with a New York socialite on his arm.

The Tenderloin would never be the same again.

Smiling, I sat back in my booth and raised a silent toast to the people in my life. My family. Those who couldn't make it and those who could: Dante, Thanh-Thanh, Darling, Katrina, Trang, Kato, Susie, even Sal.

I'd spent way too much time and energy feeling sorry for myself, calling myself an orphan, whining that nobody loved me and that I had no family.

What a fool I'd been.

As an Italian-American, I'd been raised to believe that blood is thicker than water and that nobody could ever love you like your blood relatives did. And that might be partly true, but it was also true that your family is comprised of the people you love and who love you.

We can all make our own family.

I was unbelievably rich in the love of my tribe, my family. It took almost losing my life to realize this. The people in my life were the ones I had chosen to make up my family.

It didn't mean I wouldn't love and miss my parents until the day I died. It didn't take away from my love of them. My love for my new family only increased the love I felt for everyone and everything.

When all this was over I was going to call Bobby. I needed to clean out my parents' house and then I wanted to fly to Sicily to figure out what to do with the villa Turricci had given my mother. I was going to see if Bobby would go with me. The thought of seeing him again filled me with both fear and excitement.

Maybe he didn't look at me like my father looked at my mother. Not yet. But I couldn't deny there was something there. And hey,

I'm still young and have a long time to figure it all out. I'm not going to waste any more time feeling sorry for myself when I can be out there feeling and living and loving.

<<<<<<<>>>>>>>

Keep reading for an excerpt from Gia and the Forgotten Island (A Gia Santella Crime Thriller #2).

GIA AND THE FORGOTTEN ISLAND

A Gia Santella Crime Thriller, #2

THE GRAVEYARD WAS MY sanctuary.

With nearly everyone I loved dead, it was the one place I felt at home. The only place I truly felt comfortable in my skin.

Today, I was visiting my friend Ethel Swanson's grave. I made the trip across the Bay to the Berkeley cemetery every few weeks so I wouldn't forget that she had died because of me. I had vowed—well, made a promise at her grave—that I would make sure she was never forgotten.

My favorite time to visit Ethel was at sunset, when the dipping sun made the Golden Gate bridge glow and turned the waves of the bay into sparkling silvery shimmers of light.

Yesterday, I'd driven to Monterey to put flowers on my family's graves. Pink roses for my mother. Sunflowers for my father. Nothing for my brother. I often found others had left flowers on my parents' plots. My brother's grave remained barren. His was closer to the fence and set apart from the other family plots. The grass around it was less green, more overgrown with weeds, as if even the caretakers were wont to neglect his final resting place.

His murder was still unsolved. And I didn't care.

The man who killed my parents had died at my hands. That was all that mattered.

After a cursory glance at Christopher's grave, I'd crossed my legs and sat on the grass to talk to my mother and father about my life. It was pretty much the same script every month: I told them that I was a failure, that I had moments of clarity when I stopped drinking and doing drugs, and sleeping around, but that I was still a hot mess. I told them about Bobby and our long-distance relationship. About how he seemed wonderful and how that scared the hell out of me.

Of course, I never shared like that with Ethel.

Today, I stood at her gravestone and rearranged the red roses I had delivered there every week. Once upon a time, Ethel had confessed to me how she ended up on the streets. Her jerk husband used to beat her nearly to death and then in typical abuser-fashion would beg her forgiveness by offering red roses and empty promises.

The only thing that stopped his abuse was a knife to the heart one night when he was sleeping. Years later, when Ethel was released from prison, she couldn't find work and turned to drinking. Soon, she ended up on the streets begging.

We'd become pals when I moved into the Tenderloin neighborhood and she camped outside my building.

And then, a few months ago, she'd ended up dead. Strangled with a playing card, the one-eyed jack, stuffed down her throat.

The Tenderloin newspaper ran a brief obituary.

ETHEL SWANSON had dreamed of being an actress ever since she was a little girl. She certainly had the personality and name for it. However, when she fell in love with the wrong man, her dreams were shattered, said friend Gia Santella. She never quite recovered from her abusive marriage and ended up on the streets of the Tenderloin where she was beloved by all. She died violently, but she will never be forgotten. She is buried underneath a flowering tree in the Oakland hills and has red roses delivered to her grave every week. "Because she mattered," Santella said. Ethel Swanson was 70.

As the sun set and the stars rose above, I traced my fingers over Ethel's gravestone.

"I'm sorry, Miss Ethel. I'm so goddamn sorry you're there and I'm here. It's all my fault. I wish I could make it up to you."

CHAPTER ONE

THE NEXT MORNING, DANTE side-eyed me as I stepped out of the elevator into the penthouse lobby of my father's company. Instead of his usual brilliant white smile, Dante frowned.

"What?" I asked, scowling. I was in a bad mood. Getting up at the freaking crack of dawn—okay before noon—did not suit me. The fog hadn't even lifted from my San Francisco neighborhood yet.

And meeting with stuffy board members was high on my list of things I never wanted to do in my lifetime.

But now that my father, brother, and godfather were dead, I'd been left in charge. For whatever reason, I was now the CEO. Something I had never wanted and still didn't.

The penthouse lobby looked nothing like it had when my dad was alive. It now had plush red carpet and was scattered with black onyx pedestals holding oddly familiar-shaped obelisks nearly as big as me. Two walls were covered in mirrors. I drew my gaze back to my agitated friend. While his silky black hair swept back from his face like the Italian Stallion he was, his olive skin was slightly ashen.

"What's wrong? Are you feeling okay? You look a little pale." I reached over and felt his forehead. "Yeah, you're a little clammy."

Dante let out an exasperated sigh and as always, perfectly enunciated his words. "*That* is what you are wearing?"

Spoken like a ridiculously stylish gay man. I gaped at him. Then realized he was serious.

"Sure." I knew I sounded defensive. "Why not?"

I tried not to notice the contrast between my outfit and his exquisite, custom-fit Italian suit.

Dante waited to speak until a woman in an old-fashioned black-and-white maid uniform finished dusting the obnoxious white marble sculpture near us.

"You're going to introduce yourself to the board wearing black leather pants?"

"At least I wore my nicest pair." I was starting to get angry.

He closed his eyes, clearly frustrated beyond words.

I took another look at Dante, a little worried. He *had* felt clammy. And now his face was contorted. His mouth opened and closed and his nostrils flared. Was he doing deep breathing? Counting to ten?

"And that ... that shirt," he finally said, opening his eyes. "You know they can fire you."

Good, I thought, but bit my tongue.

"Fine. I'll put on my jacket." I shrugged on my black blazer. It partially concealed my white T-shirt that said "Fuck Authority" below a picture of a skull and crossbones.

The woman was now dusting an enormous white phallic symbol right beside me.

Dante looked pained. "What about the three Armani suits I bought for you last week?"

Is that what all this was about? I'd pay him back. But I knew it wasn't that. His feelings were hurt. His unerring sense of style was offended.

I shrugged. "They're cute." *If you want to look like you have a stick up your ass.*

He made a jerking motion to pop his wrist out of his sleeve. He looked at his TAG Heuer and then glanced over at the door leading to the boardroom.

"What now? Are we late, too?" I rolled my eyes and leaned back against the mirrored wall.

He met my eyes. "We might have time for you to change. I can run you back to your place. We can be a few minutes late."

I smiled, pushed away from the wall and headed toward the boardroom door.

He winced. He knew he'd lost.

"What you don't seem to get," I said over my shoulder, "is that I don't care what they think. I don't want to be here. I don't want anything to do with running this company or the stuffy old men on the board." I knew I sounded like a pouty five-year-old and I didn't care. It seemed like the woman in the maid outfit was looking for something to do closer to us. Eavesdropping. Fine by me. I didn't care who knew what I thought.

Dante caught up to me. "Gia! You've never met any of them."

"They all stood by and let my godfather drive my father's business into the ground. They never said a word. They never reached out to me even once. And now that I'm in charge, I'm only sticking around long enough to replace every goddamn one of them."

The woman audibly gasped. We both swiveled our heads toward her and she clamped her hand over her mouth.

"Excuse me," I said, gesturing with one finger. "Come over here for a second."

Her cheeks grew red.

I stuck out my hand. "I'm Gia. What's your name?"

"Carmen."

"Nice to meet you, Carmen. I got to ask you something," I said. "Do you like wearing that outfit? Tell me the truth? I promise your job won't be affected."

"No." Her voice was quiet.

"I'm sorry I couldn't hear you."

"No, I don't like it."

"I didn't think you did. It's like *Gone with the Wind* or something."

She smiled, but still looked nervous.

"Do you like your job here?"

"*Si*. I mean yes." She nodded fervently.

"I mean, would you rather work here or say at some apartment building in Russian Hill?" *Like my building.* "I could find you a job where you have less work and more money and don't have to wear a stupid get up like that."

"I like it here, really. The uniform, no? But I like working here." She shrugged. "I do what I want. Nobody bothers me. Make my own hours."

I bit my lip thinking about. "You're being honest, right?"

"Yes."

"Okay. But the uniform has to go." I squinted at her. "What are the stuffed shirts paying you?"

She named some absurdly pithy amount. "I'll double that right now. And you can wear whatever the hell you want to work every day. If anyone says anything, tell them Gia Santella told you herself."

"Okay." She gave a small smile and slipped out a nearby door.

Dante touched my elbow. "Back to what we were talking about. You can't fire them. They are elected by the stockholders. What if there are some good men on the board?"

"If I have to be the CEO—which apparently is what my father wanted—then I'll damn well do whatever it takes to root out the rotten ones and make sure they get kicked off the board. Plus, your job is to help me do that."

"What?" his eyes grew wide. I'd asked him to be my advisor, but had never elaborated on his job duties.

"You're nice. You're nonjudgmental. If anyone can determine who is worth keeping around and who isn't, it's you. Together, we can weed out the toxic ones."

"Gia! I don't want that responsibility. Good grief."

He was so cute when he swore.

"I need your help." This time my voice was quiet. It was true. I needed Dante. I didn't want to face these men on my own.

Dante ran a hand through his hair and sighed, nodding. He was in.

But then he touched my elbow again and made a face. "Leather pants?"

"Yup." I gave him another smile. "With these pants and a senator's husband at my side, they wouldn't dare fuck with me."

"We are not married yet."

"Speaking of that, are you sure you want to get married this young? I mean, I adore Matt, but, dude, you're just a baby."

"I'm nearly twenty-five."

I put my finger on my chin. "Which means you're twenty-four."

But his twenty-four was probably like my forty. I didn't want to admit it, but Dante had acted like a mature, responsible, adult since we were twelve-years-old. The opposite of me.

"Back to your outfit," he said, raising an eyebrow.

"I'd rather talk about you." I gave him my sweetest smile. Which he ignored.

"What about the Armani? You realize they cost me a small fortune, Gia."

Now, he was just griping. He thought nothing of dropping several grand on an outfit. In that way, we were alike.

"Like I said, they're cute. I'll wear the black one to the next board meeting."

"You will?"

He sounded so damn happy.

"Sure."

I sighed. After all these years, he still believed my lies.

<<<<<<<>>>>>>>

50 percent off the first four Gia Santella books here[2].

---

1. https://www.amazon.com/Forgotten-Island-Santella-Crime-Thriller-ebook/dp/B07562K7HZ/
2. https://www.amazon.com/Gia-Santella-Crime-Thriller-Boxed-ebook/dp/B079JYTP7M/

YOUR FREE BOOK IS WAITING

"Keep your eye on this writer" - Lisa Unger, NYT bestselling author

When they made fun of her family in school, she learned karate to fight back.

But now her skills had failed her.

The attack--from someone she trusted--changed her, and her life, forever.

She was alone in the world and it was up to her to seek her own justice.

Vendetta was her destiny.

YOUR FREE BOOK HERE

YOU CAN GET THE NOVELLA FREE HERE.[3]

Or here: https://www.subscribepage.com/KristiBelcamino

3. https://www.subscribepage.com/KristiBelcamino

ALSO BY KRISTI BELCAMINO

The Gia Santella Crime Thriller Series

GIA and the Dark Night of the Soul BOOK THREE[4]

Gia and the Dark Night of the Soul[5] (Book Three)

GIA SANTELLA, THE FAST-driving, hard-drinking, karate-trained free spirit, has finally put her dark past behind her.

UNFORTUNATELY, the past isn't done with her yet.

In this suspense-filled page-turner, Gia travels from her San Francisco neighborhood to her mother's native Sicily.

4. https://www.amazon.com/Dark-Night-Santella-Crime-Thriller-ebook/dp/B0767MXG14/

5. https://www.amazon.com/Dark-Night-Santella-Crime-Thriller-ebook/dp/B0767MXG14/

There, in her efforts to seek justice for a senseless slaying, she stumbles across a complex underworld that knows more about her than she ever imagined.

She soon finds herself face-to-face with a tangled web of deep dark secrets that threaten to destroy everything she ever believed was true.

READ NOW![6]

Gia and the Lone Raven[7] (Book Four)

6. https://www.amazon.com/Dark-Night-Santella-Crime-Thriller-ebook/dp/B0767MXG14/

7. https://www.amazon.com/Lone-Raven-Santella-Crime-Thrillers-ebook/dp/B0774H5WBR/

HE THOUGHT HE COULD get away with it. He was wrong.

Gia Santella's hunt for her best friend leads her on a road trip to Mexico where she learns that there is no refuge from evil despite sunny skies and bucolic beaches.

Many Americans flee to Baja, California to escape something—the drudgery of a 9-to-5 life. An abusive husband. A hefty tax bill.

But others go there to kill.

The beauty of Baja hides dark secrets and soon Gia finds herself caught up in a group of ex-pats who like the advantages of living in a place where people can disappear without a trace and nobody bats an eye.

But then Gia comes to town. She will risk everything to save the innocent ...

ORDER NOW[8]

8. https://www.amazon.com/Lone-Raven-Santella-Crime-Thrillers-ebook/dp/B0774H5WBR/

A NOTE FROM THE AUTHOR

REVIEWS ARE THE LIFEBLOOD of this author business. Reviews, honest reviews, mean the world to me. They don't have to be fancy, either. Nobody is critiquing you on your review. And they don't always have to be five-star, either. What matters is that people are reading and have opinions on my books. I am a fairly new writer and don't have the marketing push that many other writers do that gets their books out in front of other readers.

What I do have is you.

I am unbelievably lucky to have very passionate and loyal readers who take the time to let me know what they think of my books (and sometimes even where they think I could improve).

If you liked this book, I would be extremely grateful if you could take a few minutes out of your day to leave a review HERE[1]. As I said, it doesn't need to be long or involved, anything will help. Thank you!

1. https://www.amazon.com/Gia-City-Dead-Santella-Novels-ebook/dp/B0751LCQLQ/#customerReviews

ABOUT THE AUTHOR

KRISTI BELCAMINO IS a Macavity, Barry, and Anthony Award-nominated author, a newspaper cops reporter, and an Italian mama who makes a tasty biscotti. As an award-winning crime reporter at newspapers in California, she flew over Big Sur in an FA-18 jet with the Blue Angels, raced a Dodge Viper at Laguna Seca and watched autopsies.

Her books feature strong, fierce, and independent women facing unspeakable evil in order to seek justice for those unable to do so themselves.

She shares her adventures online and through her reader's group. Join for free books, information on discounts, book recommendations, yummy recipes, and updates so you never miss a new title. Find out more here[1].

If you've read her work and want to get in touch, please do! She LOVES hearing from readers!

http://www.kristibelcamino.com[2]
https://www.facebook.com/kristibelcaminowriter/
@KristiBelcamino
kristibelcamino@gmail.com

1. https://www.subscribepage.com/KristiBelcamino

2. http://www.kristibelcamino.com/

ACKNOWLEDGMENTS

HUGE THANKS TO MY TALENTED pals, Samantha Bohrman and Cristina Pippa, who are not only amazing writers, but also stellar editors who run Manufixed.com. Check them out if you need editing.

In addition, I am incredibly grateful to—and could not do this without the members of my street team, who support me, encourage me, and keep me from looking bad in print: Sharon Long, John Bychowski, Erin Alford, Liz Cronk, Doug Cronk, Steve Avery, Emmy McCabe, Emily Goehner, Taloo Carrillo, Mimi Ryan, Christine Green, Vickie Johnson, Mikki Ashe, Beverlee Smith, Lee Elliott, Kari Isaacson, Dani Adams, Terry Welch, Mary Devries, Michelle Smith, and Anissa Kennedy! Thank you!

And huge thanks to Sarah Hanley, who is not only a breathtaking writer, but makes my covers magic!

Made in the USA
Coppell, TX
05 February 2020

15465273R00125